HEY, ZOEY

HEY, ZOEY

Sarah Crossan

BLOOMSBURY PUBLISHING
LONDON • OXFORD • NEW YORK • NEW DELHI • SYDNEY

BLOOMSBURY PUBLISHING
Bloomsbury Publishing Plc
50 Bedford Square, London, WC1B 3DP, UK
29 Earlsfort Terrace, Dublin 2, Ireland

BLOOMSBURY, BLOOMSBURY PUBLISHING and the Diana logo are
trademarks of Bloomsbury Publishing Plc

First published in Great Britain 2023

A catalogue record for this book is available from the British Library

ISBN: HB: 978-1-5266-1986-0; TPB: 978-1-5266-1982-2;
EBOOK: 978-1-5266-1985-3

2 4 6 8 10 9 7 5 3 1

Typeset by Integra Software Services Pvt. Ltd.
Printed and bound in Great Britain by CPI Group (UK) Ltd, Croydon CR0 4YY

To find out more about our authors and books visit www.bloomsbury.com
and sign up for our newsletters

For Nicola Speers

If David had been sleeping with another woman, I'd have seen the signs: longer working hours, monosyllabic conversation, his phone face-down on the countertop.

But what signs could have led me to suspect Zoey?

I thought that not wanting to touch your wife was perfectly normal.

•

My parents' generation have an alarming relationship with their televisions. My mother, born in 1950, turns off her TV along with the lights in the sitting room when she goes to bed, then turns it back on again as soon as she awakens.

It was always this way.

And in the houses of my friends growing up it was the same: a persistent stream of chatter and advertising, the automated soundtrack to our working-class childhoods.

Once I had my own home, I replaced the thrum of the small screen with a silence so pure I could hear my bare feet sticking to the wooden floors, the gulp of water pausing in the pipes as it ran towards the radiators, my breath gauzy and quick.

When I married David, I asked him to watch the football upstairs so I wouldn't have to hear the droning of the commentator. I found the repetitive rumble of our neighbour's perennial hot tub so unbearable I complained in a gently worded text message.

Silence became the goal.

Until it was the problem.

Which it always had been anyway.

My life's dream was to live in a detached house.

•

I met David at one of Leonard's parties the summer I graduated. My limbs clenched as he came into the room, and I touched the ends of my hair, foolishly dyed red from a bottle that morning. I had immediately regretted it; the top of my forehead was stained pink. He was with an outrageously tall girl who was wearing a tight rainbow dress and my first thought was how odd they looked together. She had the physique of a brawny Viking while he was lean and somewhat inconspicuous in jeans and a navy shirt, a denim jacket held tightly in one fist.

I had found myself stuck with a particularly boring university acquaintance. She was disclosing her upcoming travel plans to Mallorca – 'Leaving from Stansted because, God almighty, Heathrow is a curse,' – while I tried to tune into the more sinewy conversation David was having with a group across the room. Someone suggested that the issue of fox hunting was more complex than animal rights activists were claiming and jobs would be lost if the sport were banned. David asked what sorts of jobs, and his interlocutor replied by making a joke I couldn't hear. David laughed politely then turned and we made eye contact. He took off his glasses, cleaned them on the hem of his shirt and put them back on again without taking his gaze from me. In that moment he seemed to be asking another question, and I wanted to disappear into the wallpaper behind me. He had lovely thick eyebrows.

I excused myself and found Leonard in the garden. He was flipping food on the barbecue. 'Sorry you got stuck with Elaine,' he said. His apron was smeared in ketchup. 'I forget how dreary she is. But she's nice.' I told him she wasn't that nice, that I had purposely lost touch with her.

Steadily Leonard placed a dozen vegetable skewers beneath the spitting row of burgers and sausages. He was thinner than usual on account of a devastating break-up with the boy he'd dated since he was at school. They'd been faithful throughout university, despite living apart and Leonard being regularly propositioned by lecturers and post-grads in the English department. While the rest of us stumbled legless around the student union on a Friday night, Leonard was on a bus heading for Leeds. At the time we envied his puzzling and stubborn commitment to love. But in light of the break-up, his fidelity seemed a waste of time.

'Who's the bloke inside with the wavy hair?' I asked. 'Denim jacket. Glasses.'

Leonard asked if I fancied him. I shrugged. Back then I desperately wanted Leonard to think I embodied a level of cool indifference to anything potentially interesting. I suppose what I really felt was mild embarrassment for being so tediously straight next to his enlightened homosexuality.

He said, 'David's a junior doctor. I met him through Jason.' He began to explain who Jason was when David and the Viking stepped onto the patio. 'He's definitely in your league. But that hair is a mistake. It makes you look like you're grappling for a personality. It's the sort of thing Elaine would do.'

'Oh, fuck off.'

David followed the scent of burnt food to where we were standing. He reached for a roll and broke it open with his hands then held it out for a sausage. 'How are you, Lenny?' he asked.

The Viking had joined another group but was watching us. I sensed her examining me in particular.

Leonard looked at the sky. 'It's not pissing on my meat, so I'm alright. You?'

David nodded without answering and bit into his hot dog. His Viking was still peering at me.

'I need the loo,' I said, and went inside where I used Leonard's hand towel to rub vigorously at my forehead.

When I came back out, David had disappeared. I sat in a corner of the garden and put on my shades. Before long Elaine was next to me rattling on about the Middle East and the failures of NATO. I closed my eyes hoping she wouldn't notice through my sunglasses.

As I was leaving the party, sober because I'd driven, I finally spoke to David. He was sitting on the front step. 'I'm off,' I told him.

He looked at his watch. 'It's the weekend,' he said. I explained that I had to work the next morning.

'Shit. Me too.' He threw the end of his cigarette into the road. His eyes were bloodshot. 'You're not walking home by yourself are you?'

'I've got my car with me.'

'Oh. That's very mature.' He tilted his face towards me. 'I almost broke up with my girlfriend this afternoon.'

'Almost?' I was delighted by the revelation and sat down next to him.

'She concluded we needed to spend more time together.'

'Maybe you should try telling her again,' I suggested.

'I did. About an hour ago. What she heard me say this time was that I wanted her to go to the off-licence. I'm already totally wankered.'

'So write her a letter or send an email. You could turn your feelings into a rap.'

He smiled. 'She's alright. Uncomplicated. So maybe it'll work out.' He rooted in his pocket for more cigarettes and lit up. 'I want a simple life. Do you know what I mean?'

I worked in Zara back then, folded clothes and attended a fitting room for a living. I'd only just applied to train as a secondary school teacher and do something with my degree. I wanted a salary that would pay for a room in a shared house, so I could stop living at home, so I could choose my own bread. I already had a simple life, and I thought that to others I might seem as dull as Elaine. What I actually wanted was a bigger life, though it felt out of reach.

David's girlfriend appeared up the road. She was carrying a wine bottle in each hand. 'I'll get out of your way,' I said.

'You're not in the way. I'm David.'

'I know.'

'You know?'

'Yeah. Leonard told me. I'm Dolores.' We shook hands. His grip was certain, gentle.

•

I admit I have been a bit smug. The biggest house on the street. Low-intervention wines delivered to our front door in sustainable packaging. Handmade closets in every room and an electric awning that stretched the width of the deck and kept the kitchen cool, even during globally warmed summers. The floors were made and laid by artisans. The abstracts on the walls were originals. I knew all the artists personally.

Only the brave or stupid lift the rug, take it into the garden and beat the living shit out of it. An incident forces conflict. And change. Zoey was that change, that conflict.

Zoey.

Hey.

Hey, Zoey.

•

Intuition is science. It is what happens when the brain sees two or more incongruous details and a narrative in the subconscious cannot be established. We pause before crossing a road and barely avoid getting killed by a motorcycle, or take the stairs rather than sharing a lift with a stranger who turns out to have murdered a nun. The story told afterwards is that a mystical force from the future sent a warning in the form of a feeling. Fear as foresight. We believe we are in tune with the transcendent. But this is bullshit.

The only truth is that each sense is alive to narratives where pieces are missing, and we are very good at filling in the gaps.

So.

I know why I turned to examine the nylon bag rather than chucking the laundry into the tumble dryer and leaving. But it was only after I touched the bag that I consciously spotted the Christmas tree in pieces by the garage door, its branches arranged at odd angles. My peripheral vision must have clocked the tree and sent a signal: something is out of place.

I unzipped the bag.

Everything was wrong.

Inside was a woman with long, smooth limbs. She was about my height but she was young, her hair disarranged, her lips fleshy, eyes open.

I could smell petrol and plastic.

I felt the air around me crisp.

But I was already late leaving for work. I had only dealt with the laundry to prevent it from sitting in the washing machine all day and stinking.

I zipped up the bag, covered the woman, and kept her hidden.

Then I drove to school.

•

I tried calling Jacinta from the car. It rang and rang. Then I got through to Leonard and explained, but he couldn't figure out what I was trying to say. 'What do you *mean?*' We got cut off as his train went through a tunnel, and I couldn't connect to him again.

I fixated on the Christmas tree the rest of the way to work. I was the one responsible for its care: putting it together, taking it apart. It was a job I did on the same days each year, though I hated it. And now it was probably damaged because someone – because David – had a petrifying secret.

•

Tessa Winters was in my office for threatening another student. Tessa told the girl she would get her cousin to kidnap her and bury her alive.

'Did you really say that?' I asked.

'Yeah. So what?' She chewed gum, her legs spread, body slumped. The previous term Tessa had been suspended for smacking a tray across a former friend's face and breaking the girl's nose. The previous year she was arrested for trespassing in a maternity ward.

'What exactly did Megan Dubanowski do to provoke you to say such a thing?' I asked.

Tessa ripped tiny pieces from the corner of an exercise book with her fingernails. 'She's a bitch.'

'Well, firstly, that isn't a word I want to hear in school. And secondly, this appears to be completely unprovoked, Tessa. Her parents called and want you kicked out.' She shrugged. Her knees were scratched. Her shirt was too short at the cuff. 'Your head of year told me only last week how great you've been doing. She said you have a main part in *Bugsy Malone.*'

Tessa studied me. She knew the routine: a dressing down, a bit of approval, a punishment perhaps. But Tessa wasn't someone I needed to delude with false praise. She was a good performer, loud and funny. Despite this, Tessa never had a parent attend a performance. Sometimes her aunt saw the shows. Occasionally a friend from another school.

'We have an anti-bullying policy, and I can't make any exceptions.'

'It stinks in here.'

'Of what?'

'I dunno. Cornish pasty or something.'

'Do you even *have* a cousin, Tessa?'

'Yeah. His name's Neil. He's in prison.'

'I'm sorry to hear that.'

'His girlfriend cheated on him, so he buried her alive near Pyecombe Golf Club.'

'Is that a joke?'

'No.'

'Oh my God.'

'She never died. He'd jammed her into this massive suitcase but forgot to take off her Apple Watch, so she called her mum. She only had a broken ankle.'

•

I rang Jacinta again, but it was still the middle of the night in New York. Then I tried Mum who answered immediately. She didn't recognise my voice. I had to explain who I was. 'Did you eat the casserole I left yesterday?'

She told me she didn't like chicken and that she couldn't get the television to work without a password. 'I'll need a code to get into the microwave next.'

'Mum, please eat the casserole. And don't mess with the TV.'

She shouted: 'It has *mushrooms* in it.'

I put down the phone, and even though I'd probably be late for a meeting with the headteacher later that day, I drove to Mum's house.

She lived a few minutes' drive from my own home, in a bungalow purchased by David, as an investment, after Mum's partner Pete died, leaving her penniless.

As I let myself in, Mum appeared from the downstairs toilet carrying a mug. 'Did you wash your hands?' I asked.

'I was watering the plants in there, will you give over.' Her hair was flat at the back and greasy at the front. She had what looked like egg yolk down one side of her pilled cardigan. 'A storm's coming tomorrow and is going to last into next month. They said so on the radio. Did you hear about the raw sewage in the sea? They pumped it in at Seaford and now there's shite all along the coast from Hastings to Bognor Regis.'

I heated the casserole and we ate it together in the living room. While I was there, I filled a bag with bobbly clothes for the British Heart Foundation, and put it into the boot of my car. Mum said, 'I can do that myself, you know. I'm not useless. Shouldn't you be at work anyway? Have you lost your job?'

'No, Mum.'

'Does Jacinta have a job?'

'Yes, Mum. She's in America, remember? She paints.'

'That isn't a job.'

'It is if she makes money from it.'

'And does she?'

David called as I was pulling out of the driveway. He was breathless. 'The mortgage runs out at the end of the month,' he said. 'Would you mind calling Halifax and asking what rate we can get on another two-year fixed?'

I said, 'What?'

And he said, 'We've had an emergency here. I can't spend the day getting quotes. Do you mind?'

'I have a meeting.'

'OK. But can you call Halifax?'

I wanted to confront him about what I'd found, but I didn't know what to say. And I didn't know what I'd found. When I see him now, still when I see him, I hardly know what to say.

•

My father was what many people would call a
nice guy: affable, entertaining and entirely lacking
substance. He had a thin moustache and very bad
teeth. I have seen photographs of him when he was
younger. Always smiling because that is what you did
for a picture in the seventies and eighties: you smiled
the best version of yourself into the future and hoped
to be remembered as charming. But all his relationships were transactional, so no one really liked him
– my mother certainly didn't, and wouldn't even
pretend to for the sake of his progeny's psychological wellbeing. I never got to know my father, but
his sabbaticals from our home were an unambiguous
story: the beginning, middle and ending of all things
were about him.

His name was Seamus O'Shea; he was the son of a
wealthy dairy farmer from Donegal, though he opted
for a career in day labouring at building sites around
London. Seamus wore tracksuits and bought two-litre
bottles of cider. You'd think from his confidence and
my mother's unwillingness to leave him that he was
a catch, but he was a very average person. His accent,
however, gave him the sexy whiff of a terrorist.

Seamus regularly took us to the Wimpy in Wood
Green for dinner because he was friendly with the
manager. After our burgers and chips, Jacinta and I
were served whipped ice cream with chocolate sauce.
My father gifted the manager tools and other building supplies in lieu of payment. My mother watched

these exchanges without comment. She ordered tea and slices of toast with jam. She refused to enjoy any real dinner.

My parents argued a lot about food. I listened with my ear against the bedroom wall to their habitual shouting. They argued about traffic too. And other women.

Seamus liked Jacinta best. She knew many things and that made Dad laugh and Jacinta would give me looks that begged the question, *Is he an idiot?* I think he was a little bit of an idiot, especially compared to Jacinta.

I must have been eight or nine when Dad finally moved out for good, though apart from his dusty work boots missing from the mat in the hall, we hardly noticed. Also, Mum took a job. She hadn't worked since she lived in Dublin where she'd sold tickets from a booth in Busáras. Then she met Seamus and got married. Mum had no qualifications, but through a friend found a nannying position with a rich family in Highgate. The father was a bestselling crime author and my mother was required to keep the two young children out of earshot so he could concentrate. On one occasion – apparently he was editing his novel's climax – the children were in the garden squalling and riding their tricycles across his lawn when he hollered from the window at my mother to keep them quiet. Arriving for work the next morning, Mum found the tricycles in small, unsalvageable pieces in the middle of the lawn. She was required to say nothing about it.

We heard from my father now and then. Often on our birthdays. He was a nice guy – not someone who wouldn't keep in touch with his children.

•

We all want to believe our parents were in love. This is fantasy versus science. Procreation is a simple biological process that requires no emotion or intelligence.

•

I cannot recall a time before Jacinta. She came after me, but I only remember there being an *us,* and that didn't include Mum or Dad.

When Jacinta started school, Mum dropped us off hurriedly, handing each of us a banana, and instructing me to hold Jacinta's hand which I'd been doing since we'd left home anyway. We walked through the gates and into the reception classroom.

I said, 'This is my sister. She starts school today.'

The teacher patted my head to show me how well I'd done and said, 'You're a very big girl, Dolores. Thank you.'

Jacinta wouldn't let go of me and I didn't pull away. I let her hold on. She said, 'I would prefer to be in your class please.'

The teacher said, 'It's harder in Dolores's class. You need to learn to read and write first.'

Jacinta looked around her classroom, the large letters on the wall, the toy kitchen in the corner. She was weighing her options. Another teacher, plump and pretty, approached her with a box. 'I wish I had a helper to pass out all the crayons.'

'I can help,' Jacinta said.

I watched her take a crayon from the box, place it in front of the chair on one of the desks. And another and another, mindfully setting down each crayon. Serious. Purposeful. Then she sat at one of the desks and, on a piece of paper the teacher had given her, she wrote the words I CAN READ AND WRITE ALREADY.

•

I have a strong physical reaction to restaurants that play music too loudly or don't pay attention to the atmosphere they are creating with their playlists. I am similarly sensitive to bright lights. To succeed in the hospitality industry a basic awareness of the human senses is essential, and I base all my Google reviews on them. *The lighting made me feel like I was about to undergo dental surgery.* One star. *There is only so much Norah Jones a patron can stomach.* One star.

A restaurateur once replied to a review. He asked how customers were meant to read menus if they couldn't see them. I suggested candles for the tables. He worried these would increase his insurance premiums. I replied that life could be unfair. *Yep*, he said. I wondered at the time whether to delete the review. But I didn't.

•

For years Mum made jokes about dating a Belmarsh prison inmate. She'd say things like, 'Trevor is completely innocent,' and 'That jury was crooked,' and 'No one ever found the bodies, so what does that tell you?' We enjoyed this phantom boyfriend, a man behind bars who couldn't disturb the fine balance at home. Dad was gone, but things hadn't fallen apart. We went to school, Mum went to work, and at weekends we cleaned the house together and went to the swimming pool when Mum wasn't too tired.

Then Pete. An actual man.

He was feeding the ducks in the park when Mum pulled up next to him to admire a 'lovely mallard' on the bank of the pond. This was strange: Mum admiring nature of any kind or slowing down when we were on our way somewhere. To the post office on that particular day. She usually walked several strides ahead of us, occasionally looking back to shout, 'Get a move on.'

Pete offered us some bread from his carrier bag which Jacinta and I greedily accepted. Mum didn't stop us or insist we hurry up. She didn't mention the mud we were standing in or the state of our shoes. Jacinta threw a few crusts into the water then frowned and turned to Mum. 'Do you know him?' she asked.

'Who? No,' Mum said. But she wasn't an experienced liar at that time, so we immediately suspected that this chance encounter was staged.

'I'm Pete,' Pete said mechanically and held out a hand to Mum. She shook it and smiled. This was out of character for Mum who was wary of strangers and conclusively gave the game away: they'd met before. Pete smiled too. He had dandruff on his collar. Then he stuffed his carrier bag of bread into the pocket of his waxed jacket and said, 'A lovely day for an ice pop. You girls fancy one?'

The following week Pete was in our kitchen making himself beans on toast like he'd always been there, searching in the fridge for margarine. And not long after that, Pete's son Gavin was poking around in the fridge too. Gavin was a vegetarian when we met him, and that seemed somewhat sophisticated, although he started eating meat a few years later when he went on the Atkins diet.

They both eventually moved in, and Jacinta and I were forced to share a bedroom. I wrote a letter to Seamus O'Shea explaining the situation and asking if he was ever coming home. He didn't write back. I don't think he received the letter, sent to his

parents' farm just outside Buncrana, or if he did, he
may not have been sure which of his daughters had
written to him.

·

I worried about Jacinta who was ten to my twelve,
twelve to my fourteen, fourteen to my sixteen.
I watched for warning signs that she was afraid or
angry or mute. I followed her around the house to
make sure she wasn't concealing anything and, when
she was in her teens, checked her arms for cuts. She
said, 'Please stop looking at me.' I hadn't thought
she'd noticed. She said, 'What did I do wrong?' I
wanted to squeeze her, tell her to be careful, but how
could I have done that without eliciting questions?
So I smacked her hard across the face and told her
not to be such a baby. She held her hot cheek, three
fingermarks clearly visible, and in a small, confused
voice said, 'I'm sorry, Doughy.' I could see that she
was sorry, but it was too late for me to retract the
hurt. I stormed into the garden and feverishly ripped
out the bindweed strangling the plants – Pete gave
us pocket money for helping to pull weeds – and
as Jacinta watched through the window, I knew she
was checking through a list in her head of possible
offences and coming up blank. The next day I gave
her my share of cherry trifle, but she couldn't finish
it and my offering ended up in the bin.

•

When Jeremy Ashworth took over as headteacher, he chose an office as far from student congregating points as possible. The prior head taught a couple of times each week and even did a lunch duty. Jeremy was too busy focusing on marketing and publicity and on the future of the school, he said, to be involved with trivialities. He had a tan, even in winter.

At the meeting he greeted me with a half-wave and told me there was no need to sit. He was pleased to reveal that permission for a new sports hall had been approved by the council's planning department. The next stage would be to gather tenders from construction companies. A letter to parents would be sent out as soon as possible.

His office was spotless, most of the shelves empty. I asked whether he'd thought any more about employing a full-time nurse. He shook his head. 'We're going to get more staff trained as first aiders.' I asked if he'd reconsidered allocating a budget towards the staff social at the end of term. 'No,' he said. He said, 'Did you go out for lunch today? Your car's moved.'

'Yes.'

'Did you report to the office that you'd be off-site?'

'Yes.'

'Right.'

'Is there a problem, Jeremy?'

'No. No problem.'

I could see the traces of fake tan between his
fingers.

•

After school I slipped into the garage and unzipped
the bag a few inches. The woman was where I had
left her, eyes reflecting the slice of light coming in
through the side door. And a memory came to me,
though I thought it was my imagination, a brain blip.

Darkness and noise and a stinging sensation. The
smell of spring onion.

Bile in my throat had me running for the house
where I was sick in the kitchen sink.

Bits of casserole from lunch clogged the plughole.
Visible chicken chunks and slithers of mushroom.

•

Not long ago I attended a TEDx talk by an Estonian
journalist and researcher who wore over-the-knee
leather boots. It was my focus, as she spoke, the way
she paraded in those heels like she'd always been on
stage, graphs with unlabelled x and y axes behind her
on a big screen. She advised the audience to trade in
our phones, laptops and smart watches for books and
meaningful conversation, for long walks and medi-
tation. She told us that the human being has lost its
ability to pay attention, that deep thinking is being

hindered by our attachment to the speed of technology. The audience applauded, I amongst them. She had impressed me. I decided I would buy a copy of *Middlemarch* or *Dracula* and use the rest of the week for reading. But instead I went home and searched online for a pair of high boots. I spent the week breaking them in.

•

I was in bed by the time David got home. He came into the room, asked about the mortgage, was pleased I'd dealt with it so efficiently, and fell asleep within a few minutes. His back was hairier than it had ever been. His shoulders were peppered in moles the size of my thumbnails. I'd told him more than once to get them checked. Surely he knew a dermatologist.

I missed him that night, fearing our relationship was over, fearing that the man I married never existed, that the benign David I knew was a person of my own creation while the real David was someone else entirely.

Even before I gave him a chance to explain, I worried that I wouldn't ever see him in the same way again.

•

David wasn't my first lover. I slept with someone a month after arriving at university, a Cypriot in my halls of residence. He was a little older on account of his mandatory military service. Leonard and I called him sexy lips. He hadn't much to say, but the way he smoked and hardly moved as he danced made me nuts. We had sex in his room one Sunday afternoon. My mum and Jacinta had been for a visit and left me iced buns and bottles of Fanta which I took to him as an offering once they'd left. I told him I was a virgin as he was pulling down my knickers, ripping the lace band a little, kissing and sucking on my chin. His pillow smelled stale and there were socks and pants balled up all around the room. Afterwards he said, 'You lied. No virgins fuck like that.' I picked up my shoes, left his room and went to sleep in my own bed a few doors along the corridor, not knowing whether to be flattered or insulted.

Then I slept with the Cypriot's best friend a few times, mostly because he had a car, so I didn't have to haul my own groceries home from the supermarket every week. I bought a lot of tinned foods which were heavy. We drove through car washes for fun, used the time to kiss and put our hands into one another's clothes. I soon worked out that it didn't matter which program you purchased – bronze, silver, gold, platinum – they all essentially did the same thing and lasted six-and-a-half minutes. It was enough time to get turned on but not enough to see any adventure through to completion.

I began my second year by sleeping with my genetics lecturer, but when his wife found out and threatened to destroy me, I decided to find myself an actual boyfriend. Craig was studying industrial engineering. He also wrote a lot of long nature poems I couldn't understand. He asked me to type them up for him while he looked into the horizon or drank strong coffee. I wore tulle and went with him to author readings. He dumped me for a hockey girl with a loud laugh and a gum shield.

Studying for my exams in the library at midnight, I met Mitchell. I downplayed my feelings for my previous lovers. I told him that Craig had been a chauvinist and lazy in bed. Then I told him that the others had all been mildly abusive, especially the lecturer. The way a good man responded to the idea that a bad man had mishandled me – with concern then outrage – I found appealing. Carefully Mitchell asked questions: 'So did he do that all the time? Did you mind? Did you enjoy it even a little bit? I think you can only enjoy that sort of sex when you're in love, you know?' Mitchell felt we had a deep connection and so, the very thing I told him I'd been coerced into doing with everyone else, I began doing with him. I'd beg for it while he whispered my name in the darkness along with the words, 'I love you. Oh, I love you. Thank you. Thank you, Dolores.'

I stayed mostly celibate after Mitchell, until David, of course. David with his clean bedsheets and post-coital cups of tea. After our first time together, he cleared out a drawer and told me I could leave my things in it. He ran baths for me and made cheesy omelettes when he had time.

Before that I had leaned into Leonard. 'Don't you get horny though, babes?' he asked. I didn't. In my late teens and early twenties I rarely thought about sex. Mostly I wanted to be untouched. I went back into halls in my third year and liked the safety of a locked room at night.

•

For a long time I hated Pete and Gavin living with us. They changed the smell of the house. They owned a lot of stuff and made every room feel cluttered. But eventually there were benefits. Gavin took me to my first concert, Blur, balancing me on his shoulders as I swayed and sang. And when I thought Alex James looked directly at me and cried, Gavin hugged me and said he'd be crying too if it had happened to him. I was twelve and in love with Alex James and Damon Albarn. I was in love with loads of grown-ups by then, including most of Gavin's friends, even the short, spotty ones.

Jacinta was at home that night. She was too young to come with us and mostly too young to be friends with Gavin, which suited me. I liked having him and his world to myself. And Jacinta had a new friend anyway – Hilary Russo, a girl with a round, red face and ginger hair who I found particularly ugly. I worried at the time that associating with such a face would cause other children to shun my pretty sister, but that never happened. The two of them wrote letters to one another almost daily, even after they'd spent the day side-by-side at school. Jacinta skipped to the letterbox at the end of our road in the evenings with a thick envelope and squawked with excitement whenever post arrived in the mornings from Hilary, the address barely legible, the postcode missing.

I admit I was a little jealous of Hilary, this word-smith who ignited a kind of euphoria in my sister, but I focused on Gavin. I knew he viewed me with a detached, teacherly interest, loaning me CDs and copies of *NME* and even his penknife.

Pete encouraged our friendship at first, viewing his son's generosity as an extension of his own goodness, but this quickly turned into mild mistrust. He warned Gavin that he was not, under any circumstances, to give me alcohol or cigarettes. Mum repeated this warning. And they both told Jacinta that they would *not* continue to supply her with first-class stamps unless she made her bed every morning and helped with the dishes.

Jacinta did neither of these things, yet the letters continued both ways for almost another year.

I never asked her where the stamps came from.

•

People die in operating rooms where David is the consultant anaesthetist. They also die in recovery hours later. He has never seen these as personal losses. He has said, 'My job is to give the surgeon time to fix the body. If the body can't be fixed, there's nothing I can do about that.'

I asked him if it ever made him sad. 'Yes,' he replied.

'Does it hurt when someone you're trying to keep alive can't be helped?'

'I do my best, and I hope for the best,' he told me. And I could understand this. For the most part David was good and hoped for good things to happen. He exercised and felt this was his contribution towards warding off ill health. He saved a little of his earnings each month in the belief that compound interest would pay off. He said regret was a pointless emotion. He said he wasn't an executioner in Texas. He said he had to attend a summit in California. He said he couldn't sleep and got up to make himself toast. He burnt the toast and the smoke detector went off. We hired an electrician who fitted a less sensitive alarm.

David was not often home alone.

So when?

How can I have missed it?

Regret is a pointless emotion.

•

Jacinta and I shared a doll. I don't know where it came from, but it wasn't from a shop because by the time we adopted her, she was missing her shoes and socks. We named her Grace. She had long, curly hair until Jacinta cut it short and I cut it even shorter. We scribbled nonsense on her body with felt tips and tried to rub it off with cotton balls soaked in nail varnish. We fought over her so hard, Jacinta at one end, me at the other, we pulled her head clean off and agreed to play separately with the two parts of her until Mum found a way to reattach the decapitated head saying, 'You can forget about a hamster.'

•

The second time I bumped into David was a few years after the barbecue. I'd moved back to London from Cambridge where I'd done my teacher training, and was in an Islington bar for Leonard's homecoming: he was back from a stint in Quebec and working as an assistant to an editor at a children's publishing company. He was making less money than anyone I knew at the time but never let me pay for anything. He'd say, 'I'm busy and often volatile. Money is the only way I can contribute to your life right now, darling.' He was dating a well-known actor but intermittently despairing of their non-monogamous arrangement.

David tapped me on the shoulder. His hair was longer, tucked behind his ears, and up close his eyes seemed very big behind his glasses. 'Dolores? We met at Leonard's party. I'm David.' I had been reintroduced to a few of Leonard's friends that night and each of them pretended not to remember me, or perhaps they really didn't remember me.

'How did it go with the break up?' I asked. He said he had gone out with the Viking for another month. 'Then she gave me the push. Took my car in for a service and met a mechanic who serviced her too. I know it sounds like the opening scene to a bad porno.'

'I wasn't aware there was good porno.'

'Right.'

'Huh?'

'I didn't say anything.'

David had come with a friend who handed him a bottle as he joined us. He put out his hand. 'Pierre,' he said. He had light brown skin and a little snake tattooed onto his collar bone.

'Pierre's in oncology,' David said. I made noises of respect, but I wasn't all that impressed. I'd met enough medics to know they were secretly derisive of anyone not in medicine; somewhere deep down they were still gloating about their impressive A-level results.

I asked David what he did, though I already knew. 'Anaesthesiology,' he said weakly, like this was a confession. He chugged his beer and added, 'Leonard told me you're a teacher. What subject?'

'Only psychos do anaesthesiology,' Pierre interrupted. 'And imbeciles go into psychology. Or become GPs.'

David shook his head. 'Pierre's elected to take a job in Pennsylvania. He isn't interested in our great and good National Health Service.'

'I want to be rich!' Pierre said. He laughed, but from the look of the suede loafers he was wearing and the gold bracelet on his wrist, I assumed there was a truth to it.

'My mum taught for twenty years, but she's retired already,' David said.

Pierre was scanning the room for someone more interesting to engage with. David was still waiting for me to speak.

'I teach biology and chemistry,' I said quietly. I felt glaringly unremarkable standing there in an ill-fitting dress I'd borrowed from Jacinta, very flat shoes. I wanted to have a story to tell David to keep him from walking away and considered starting at the beginning with the words, 'When I was about twelve years old...' but David didn't go anywhere. He asked questions about my family and my job and my hobbies and my favourite books because he wasn't scouting for shocking tales of woe and trauma and intrigue. Not then. Not ever. As he'd said the first time we met, 'I want a simple life.' And he lured me into that life because I thought David might be the one to transform me from something defective into something normal.

Later that night we were doing shots with Leonard when David said, 'I have to head off, lads. I've got an early shift. But do you wanna go out one evening next week maybe?'

Leonard, completely blotto, licked David's cheek. 'I've been hoping you two would get it on.' We stood awkwardly for a few seconds, and I was expecting David to add that it wouldn't be a date. But when he didn't, I gave him my number.

'Is he a mental person?' I asked Leonard when David had gone. Leonard frowned. His boyfriend was on the way with coke and a strange man. 'He seems so…' I couldn't explain how David made me feel, but it was close to adequate.

Leonard pushed me. 'He's a fucking doctor, babes. A *doctor*. And every time I talk to him, he asks about you.'

'What?'

Leonard shrugged like this was baffling to him too. 'He's not into girls with massive tits and big personalities.'

'I have tits.'

Leonard looked at my chest. 'Yeah. You do.'

•

After I'd had a cup of tea and called Mum to make sure she hadn't fallen or set the curtains on fire, I took another look. 'Hello? Hello?' I whispered. She did not reply. Her mouth was slightly open. I put my fingers to the lips. They were soft and gave a little as I pressed my nails against them. 'Hello?'

Her aliveness was a ruse.

Though she wasn't dead either.

She was a trick.

She was a toy.

●

Agalmatophilia from the Ancient Greek άγαλμα meaning 'statue' and φιλία meaning 'love', is sexual attraction to a doll or mannequin – it's a thing. I looked it up. Rather than confronting my husband, I engaged in some internet research.

2

I know shame cannot be a vehicle for change. I should sit David down and say, 'I'm not angry, I'm disappointed,' like I would with a student who'd messed up. But this isn't true. I'm so angry I want to spit at him. I want to pull a knife from the kitchen drawer and stab him repeatedly. I want to humiliate him. I want to tell everyone what he hid from me and have it reveal who he is and what he will always be.

•

I played with dolls far longer than was socially acceptable, and at a certain age had to carefully choose the friends I might be able to trust to visit my house. Some wouldn't have cared about me lining up my dolls along the bed in size order, but some would have held this knowledge as a weapon to be stored and used in whatever social drama was playing out.

By eleven I had only one friend, Elizabeth, who I dared invite over. I realised she was safe because after a school concert one evening her mother told my mother that Elizabeth had asked Santa for a Mr Frosty for Christmas. I was jealous, wondering whether Elizabeth would really be gifted something so frivolous. At break time I said, 'I can't believe you still believe in Santa.' I could have announced this in front of a group, but I said it quietly, as we queued for lunch.

'Shut up,' she said.

'Your mum said so.'

'You have to let them think you believe to get better presents.'

I didn't know this, and guessed it was why Mum revealed the savage truth when I was only five years old.

'I bet you asked for a doll too,' I said, warily.

'Yes! Winter's Eve Barbie. Have you seen her?' I hadn't. I needed to get a copy of the latest Argos catalogue. I invited myself over to her house later that week.

Instead of clothes inside Elizabeth's wardrobe, there were ratty pieces of tiny furniture made from egg boxes and yoghurt tubs. This was an opportunity to sneer and win tokens to buy her loyalty, but I was too impressed by what she'd created to be mocking. We played with her makeshift doll's house for hours using different voices for each doll, dressing and undressing them over and over, making them argue, threaten, placate and acquiesce. I wished that we had had a Ken doll to torture and complain about.

After that day, Elizabeth and I took turns visiting one another's houses, playing with our dolls and even sharing them. I preferred this to playing with Jacinta who was too young to keep up with the complexity of the dolls' relationships. And I learned about sex from playing with Elizabeth, when she lay one on top of another and rubbed them against each other until something mystical happened to make them stop. Elizabeth also suggested we get them to kiss one another's privates. This seemed entirely pointless to me, but we did it anyway, and then I wanted to do it every time we played together. Elizabeth would say, 'Why doesn't my one have a car crash and almost die?' And I'd say, 'And then mine is so upset they start cuddling.'

I can't remember when we stopped these games, but I know we smoked our first cigarette together, in the middle of the night, with my bedroom window wide open and Jacinta asleep on the floor. I didn't inhale, but I've never enjoyed a cigarette more than that one. Not in my whole life.

Elizabeth left school after getting ten very good GCSEs and knocked up by a local butcher. She'd had four children with him by the time I started teaching.

•

After getting my number at Leonard's get together, David called and asked if I liked the theatre. I told him I did, though I'd only ever been to see *Cats* and a couple of pantomimes. He said an older cousin of his was in a production of Berkoff's *Kvetch* and he had some comps if I was interested. 'We could eat afterwards. I don't recommend dinner beforehand as the performance may cause mild nausea.'

'Surely you have meds for that.'

'I do have access to a lot of drugs yes. Will you come?'

I wore a red dress with a thin gold thread in the fabric and wedge heels. I'd imagined a swish evening. I didn't want to show myself up. But when I arrived and saw the state of the place – a run-down grey façade next to a boarded up letting agency – and David himself dressed in jeans and an old pair of trainers, I realised I looked ridiculous. I wanted to turn around and run home. It was the sort of thing Mum or Pete would have done – not understood the tone of an occasion – and the sort of thing Jacinta and I would have been mortified by. I worried that David would think I was ignorant and common.

But he waved and half-leapt towards me. 'You look great,' he said. 'I'm a vagabond.' He opened his jacket to show me a ratty T-shirt beneath. 'I was trying to be cool. I shouldn't do that. It rarely works out.'

I wasn't sure whether he was genuinely self-conscious about his clothing or whether he was trying to make me feel better about the gaudiness of mine. Either way, I relaxed. He kissed my cheek lightly. 'This is going to be diabolical. I'm sorry. I would simply ask that you slit your wrists *after* the show, not in front of the performers.'

He was funny. And he was polite. And the play was funny. And his cousin was polite. Her name was Freya and she made David promise to bring me along to every show she was ever in because I was the most attentive audience member in the stalls, she said. The dress circle was empty. She was thankful I had laughed in all the right places, and that I hadn't been distracted by the stage manager's galling whispers. 'Plus, you're beautiful,' she said. 'And we value an attractive audience.'

No one had ever called me beautiful. I knew I was attractive enough to pull in wolf whistles and dates, but beautiful was not what I was. Beauty was a thing possessed by people with elegance, with innocence. Or something like that.

At the Cantonese restaurant on Upper Street, David told me he'd not been able to forget about me since we'd met at Leonard's barbeque years before. 'And the only reason I went to the bar in Islington was to see you.'

'Sadly you had a girlfriend when we first met.'

He nodded. 'I was scared of her and you were nice to me when everyone else told me not to be such a pussy. She was from Hull and could have wrestled me to the ground. She *would* have on a few occasions, if I'd not squirmed my way out of it.' I laughed, but I doubted this. David was slim but not weedy: until he'd left university, he'd been a rower. His wrists were toned.

He searched the dish in front of him with a fork until he found a slither of bok choy and popped it into his mouth. 'I would have asked you out, if she'd not been there that night.'

'You hardly spoke to me.'

'I tried to. You ran away. Leonard said you were embarrassed about your hair or something.'

'You're misremembering.'

'Or you're restructuring the past.' He laughed and so did I.

'I lie every day,' I said. 'It's not some nefarious thing, but I've noticed I tell these little lies to avoid hassle, to get out of meeting a friend for tea or to explain why I'm returning a pair of shoes I don't like. I suppose everyone does it. And every job requires it to some extent. You can't be a teacher and tell the truth. Can you imagine? I'd have to admit to my entire class of Year Tens that they're going to fail their exams and end up on benefits.'

'Have you lied to me?' he asked earnestly.

'No. I don't think so. Wait, yes, I have. I was very embarrassed about my hair when we met.'

The waiter came to clear our plates and we moved on to lighter topics: the best dive bars in North London; controversial Oscar wins; the pointlessness of changing the clocks twice each year. We talked whenever we had something to say and the silences were easy. David kept his eyes on me the whole night. He didn't make me nervous or feel I had to say the right thing. I ate all my dinner and ordered a dessert.

Walking me to the tube station, he took my hand. 'Marry me,' he said.

'Alright,' I agreed.

It was a joke. Of course, it was a joke. But he asked me the same question again eighteen months later and it wasn't a joke. And I gave the same reply.

Alright.

•

Our first kiss was in a train carriage. We were on our way to a Camden comedy club, standing and squished up against not only each other, but fellow passengers, the space becoming more congested at every stop. My chest was next to his, my mouth close to his ear. It was early evening. A lot of people were loud and drunk, which always made me nervous, especially if I was with a date. Nothing is more appealing to a drunk man than a sober man, especially a tall one. David was also the kind of handsome I imagined lesser men envied.

I said, 'We should have taken a taxi.'

He said, 'If we had, I'd have kissed you already.'

I said, 'Kiss me now.'

'OK.'

He put his lips against my neck and it felt like the most erotic thing that had ever happened to me. I glanced at the woman behind him who looked away, mildly disgusted. I took an awkward step backwards, into a teenager wearing headphones, and David kissed my mouth. He tasted of nothing. Not cigarettes or beer or onions or coffee. It was like I could imprint myself onto him through his lips, like both of us had just been born.

I wanted to ask him to marry me. As a joke.

•

Leonard called me at work. 'I can't talk,' I said. I had a maths class to cover plus a child in my office with a headache he was claiming might be a brain hemorrhage. His grandfather had died from one a week earlier.

'David sent the thing to me,' Leonard said.

I turned in my desk chair so I was facing the window and not the hypochondriac student. 'What?'

'The bloody doll. He had it delivered to my office. He told me it was a telescope. He said he couldn't send it to your house because you guys were away in Hertfordshire for someone's birthday and the hospital wouldn't accept personal deliveries.'

'When?'

'Like seven or eight months ago.'

'Seven or eight *months*?'

'Did you even go to Hertfordshire?'

'We go all the time to see his family, but we never stay over.'

'Fucking hell.'

'Fifteen years, Leonard,' I hissed. 'I've been with this person for fifteen years. What am I meant to do now?'

The child behind me coughed and said, 'Miss, can I call my mum?'

I turned to him. 'There's nothing wrong with you, Stewart. You probably need a glass of water.' He looked like he might cry.

Leonard said, 'I'm pissed off too, to be honest.'

'Why?'

'He bullshitted me, Dolores. Fucking lying weasel.'

'Yeah,' I replied, as Stewart scampered out of my office. He'd left his phone on the floor. I put it into my drawer and went to cover the maths lesson.

•

I thought I had experienced love before I met David, that the panic which came from waiting for a man to like me, call me, pick me, was the definition of passion. Once David came along I wasn't sure; I looked back at my previous romances with suspicion. With David there was no holding off or holding back. He called when he said he would, showed up early rather than late for dates and told me matter-of-factly how he was feeling about our relationship, which invariably was satisfied. He offered to pay for meals out but when I told him it was my turn, he put away his wallet and let me have my dignity. At night, without him, I felt no loving ache in my body. My mind was storm-free, and I slept quickly and well. I was determined to keep him. To see what it all meant.

·

When Jacinta wouldn't pick up, I was forced to text her a summary of the situation. She called back immediately. 'I don't get it,' she said. In the background loud horns and roaring engines. I assumed she was on her way to the studio.

'What don't you get?'

'Any of it. Explain from the beginning.'

'There is no beginning, Jacinta. It's what I told you. Two days ago I found a silicone sex doll in the garage, and I am quite certain I wasn't the one who put it there.'

'But *David*?'

'Yeah.'

'If it was an affair with another woman then…'

'I know.' It wouldn't have been easier, but it would have been something I could have understood. 'A part of me wants to find it funny,' I said.

'It isn't funny,' Jacinta shot back. 'Not at all.'

I described the doll to her and she sighed and tutted and said, 'Oh for the love of fuck.' Then she said, 'Catch him in the act. That's what I'd do.'

'Jacinta.'

'I don't mean actually doing it. Jesus. I mean going into the garage. If he's in there for longer than what, three minutes, you know what he's up to.'

'Three minutes? It would take at least that amount of time get her out of the bag and into a comfortable position.'

'Fine. Five minutes. You have security cameras. Use them.'

She was right. We had several cameras installed after our neighbours were broken into and their car keys stolen. The thought of a stranger invading my home while I was in bed was something I couldn't handle.

'I'm not sure that's necessary,' I said.

'It's entirely necessary. Your issue when you finally confront him will be a lack of evidence. Anyone can deny anything without it.'

•

I believed in the law of attraction, the idea I could manifest a reality if I learned to focus positive thoughts towards my goals. I had some vague notion that my mind was in part responsible for a promotion at work, my loud neighbours moving to another city, and meeting David.

David and I had been dating a few months when I explained the theory to him. We were in bed, had just had very quick sex. We were having a lot of quick sex at that time, mostly because David worked long hours and if we didn't, we wouldn't have had sex at all.

'You're not serious,' he said.

'There's something to it. You need to watch the film.'

'No, I really don't. Because by that rationale, if I want a plane to crash, I only need to use my mind to bring it down. It would make the 9/11 suicide terrorists feel a bit silly.'

'You're making *me* feel silly.'

'I'm not trying to, my sweet,' he said. 'But you're a *scientist.* I know you can't have fallen for that claptrap. You're too clever.'

'I'm a scientist. Exactly. I'm talking about neuro-science, psychology, cognition. The way we direct our thoughts impacts the outcome because it causes us to take particular actions and it moves us unconsciously towards our intentions.'

'But just because I want a little boy who's been operated on to survive cancer doesn't mean he will.'

'What little boy?'

'No little boy. It's an example.'

'Is there a little boy who has cancer?'

David sighed and kissed my nose. His lips were cold, chapped. 'There are lots of little boys with cancer.'

He was right. So I began to think about this, and steer my mind away from driving a Mercedes, and towards those little boys getting well again. I didn't believe in magic. But I did believe in some things I couldn't explain.

·

I started telling people that Gavin was my brother quite soon after he moved in because it made Mum and Pete happy when we pretended we had always been a family. This effectively erased my real father, which wasn't a problem for me.

I told David the same thing when we met. 'I have two siblings. A little sister, Jacinta, and an older brother, Gavin.'

Even so, David never liked Gavin. Before he knew much about him, and before he knew we weren't related by blood, he told me that Gavin's openness was a veneer, that his laughter hid a darkness. He found him double-sided: watchful one minute, matey the next. It made celebrations awkward, David's commitment to these cynical feelings. I tried very hard to explain that Gavin was complicated, that he'd been abandoned by his mother as a child and had a vacuous, high functioning drunk for a father.

But David does not live in nuance. There is science and faith, fact and fiction, good and evil, innocence and blame.

I knew very early on in our relationship that there were some things I would always have to keep from David, some things he would never understand.

Leonard judged all his relationships on whether or not he felt he could be intimate with the men he met. I said, 'What does that even mean?'

'It means letting someone sees bits of you that are normally kept hidden.'

'I doubt you hide your bits,' I told him.

He hadn't the energy to argue with me. But it did make me wonder about honesty and love and whether omissions were lies. How could they be? How could we possibly tell another person everything about ourselves? It would take a lifetime. It would be incredibly boring.

•

When they were both alive, David's parents lived in a cul-du-sac in St Albans. My first impression as we pulled up outside the semi-detached property where he had spent his entire childhood was how civilised it was. The blue front door had little panes of stained glass and there were red geraniums in pots along the driveway. Not one weed or scrap of moss bled between the pathway's paving stones.

His mother came out to meet us and seemed very pleased that I'd brought an apple pie for dessert.

His parents nodded with raised eyebrows as we ate our chicken tagine, a dish I'd never heard of before, and I told them about the students I taught and my sister's fine art degree. His father helped to clear the dishes and his mother smoked a cigar in the living room while we drank filtered coffee and ate the pie I'd brought.

When his younger brother Hugo arrived and invited us to a gig he was playing that night in Edgware – Hugo was the frontman with a band he'd formed at Oxford University – both parents gleefully encouraged us to attend, explaining that their youngest son was going to be the next Mick Jagger. Hugo said, 'I'm focused on process rather than success right now.'

David rolled his eyes, though not unkindly. 'We have work tomorrow,' he said. 'Another time, yeah?' He was so cordial, like Hugo was a work colleague and not his little brother.

And Hugo responded with equally good manners. 'No worries. I know you're crushed at the hospital.'

Before we left, I went upstairs to use the bathroom and accidentally opened several bedroom doors until I found the loo. Each room was painted lavender, the beds adorned with floral cushions. They had the smell of used spaces, not spare rooms as I'd have expected.

On the car ride home I said, 'Do your parents share a bedroom?' We were at a set of traffic lights.

David stalled the car and had to restart it. 'Why are you asking?'

'Just wondered.'

'I don't think so. They never did, even when I was kid.'

'Why not?'

'It's how it is. Mum gets hot at night. Dad wakes up early to read the paper.' He turned on Radio 4 and we listened to a segment about the challenges facing working mothers.

I looked out of the passenger window. The car next to us was a green Jaguar. The woman at the wheel was in her fifties and seemed angry about something the driver in front of her was doing or not doing. She turned to me for a moment and I smiled, but she didn't smile back.

We were almost at South Mimms when David spoke again. 'No one in my family has ever been divorced. Not even separated. Not one uncle or aunt or cousin. Anyone who got married stayed married. Isn't that something?' He turned off the radio and began to hum, opening the window to let the air in.

'Bloody hell,' I said. 'There must be a lot of very unhappy marriages in your family.'

Back at his flat, David hung up his coat and said, 'Shall we get a take-out later? I can't be bothered to go to the supermarket.' This wasn't like him at all. He relished an errand, a quick trip out to buy milk or fish or sesame oil, and coming home with a treat for me: a bag of chocolate buttons or a packet of malted milk biscuits.

'OK,' I said. 'I can pick it up.'

'I have an early, so it isn't worth you staying over. I'll drive you home after we've eaten.'

'Did I upset you?' I asked.

'I'm not upset. Do I look upset?'

'Yes.' The muscles in his face were tense. And he didn't seem to know what to do with his hands. 'Look, David, everyone is a little bit fucked up. You've met my family.'

'Your family aren't that fucked up.'

I could have disagreed with him, elaborated. I said, 'Maybe you're right.'

'Look, I'm fine,' he said.

'Truthfully, it makes me like you more. Knowing your family isn't perfect.'

He smiled warmly for a few seconds, and I sensed he was allowing himself to be seen. It was a rare thing. But I offered nothing in return. He sighed. 'Please stay over. I didn't mean it. I was being a dickhead. Work is stressful. I'm tired.'

This wasn't true: he had confronted something unpleasant about his parents' relationship, his own childhood, and wanted a way to explain away the disagreeable feelings before they ambushed him. And it was his right: to face whatever it was he was feeling, or turn from it.

'I'm afraid we'll end up like them. We won't, will we?' he asked.

'God no,' I said.

He put his arms around me. 'You're right. And with the way London house prices are going, we'll never be able to afford a place with two bedrooms anyway!'

•

I don't remember the exact day my dad left, but I do remember that Mum got us a grey whippet-mix from Battersea Dogs' Home to distract us from the experience. Jacinta wouldn't stop asking questions about where Dad was, when he was coming back and who he was with. She wasn't distressed. She just wanted answers. So Mum said that in exchange for an end to the investigation, Jacinta would get to name the dog.

She went for Timothy. She said Timothy was the name of a boy in her class with blue eyes and the dog reminded her of him.

'What about Bruno?' I asked. 'Or Ash.' It felt like an unparalleled opportunity to be creative and Jacinta was wasting it. But she wouldn't budge on Timothy, not even to Tim or Timmy, so though I adored that dog, I was embarrassed calling him back when we went to the park, which, to be fair, wasn't all that often. It was the name you'd give a man. And not just any man; a man from Surrey who wore pink slacks and striped T-shirts.

At first Jacinta didn't like to leave Timothy alone. Whenever we went out, she'd have a meltdown if we were gone too long. Mum said, 'It's a dog, Jacinta. Remember that. It's a feckin' dog.'

Within a few months of us getting him, Timothy died of an infection after biting his own tongue. I was sobbing uncontrollably in the car as we drove home from the vet. Jacinta took my hand in her own and said quietly, 'Try not to cry. It was a dog, Dolores. Just a feckin' dog.'

•

I didn't think David was a monster. The furthest my mind could stretch to was that he was depraved, yet I hated that word and what it said about me and my righteousness because that's not who I was. I was a liberal in the real sense of the word – not a far-left maniac who couldn't see the humanity of anyone less far-left than themselves. If I could forgive serial killers for being less fortunate than I was, I was prepared to grant an amnesty to any friends who still voted Tory.

David had always been a socialist. Even when he started to make serious money. He signed up when fundraisers knocked at the door and worried about the state of the care system. He volunteered at a women's domestic violence shelter for over five years.

So depraved seemed an unfair assessment.

What had he done anyway, apart from stick his penis into something? It wasn't a patient or a prostitute or, God forbid, a child. It was a toy and half the population had something similar hidden in a bedside drawer. I owned one, though the battery had gone and I'd lost the charger.

I Googled for an answer to my dilemma and found an article on micro-cheating. Small deceptions. Minor indiscretions. What harm if no one knows?

I thought about the fact that we are specks racing through space and the luck of consciousness seems to make everything meaningless anyway.

I got on with emailing parents and I told myself to relax.

•

In the same way we rarely mentioned Seamus O'Shea, Pete and Gavin didn't talk about Gavin's mother. All I'd heard was that she'd run off with a tree surgeon when Gavin was six, leaving Gavin alone in the house for several hours with a letter addressed to his father.

Then, one day, a phone call came. I heard raised voices in the garden, Pete waving one arm wildly and shouting into his first ever mobile phone as though it were a walkie-talkie. Gavin looked up from the beet-root he was grating and said, 'What a cunt.'

We were alone in the kitchen. Gavin was making himself a raw energy salad for lunch. I was boiling pasta for the rest of us. 'Your dad?' I asked.

His eyes flashed. 'Mum.'

'Oh.' I wanted to know more but Pete had put his phone away and was coming back into the house.

'What does she want?' Gavin asked.

'She wants her beach towels back,' Pete said.

'What beach towels?'

'I don't know what ruddy beach towels, Gavin.'

Pete pointed at the pan on the hob. 'No one likes mushy pasta,' he said.

I used a fork to taste it and the boiling water that hadn't drained from the little tube of penne burnt my tongue. It was still crunchy. Gavin reached for a red onion and began to finely chop it. He cleared his throat. 'Did she ask about me?'

Pete was looking into the bowels of our house, seemingly transfixed by the bare lightbulb hanging from the hall ceiling. His mouth was turned down. I'd never seen him cry, but he looked like he might. He must have been about forty-five then. I thought he looked like an old man. Someone with a terribly sad history. Someone who didn't have long left. 'She got cut off,' he said. 'I cut her off.'

Gavin nodded. 'She didn't even...'

'No, Gavin.' He turned to his son. They were rarely gentle with one another, but on that day Pete's voice was soft. And he said, 'That salad looks alright. Can we share it?'

•

There is nothing as irritating as a returning student who shows up during the school day *to say hello*. The actual reason for the visit is always to peacock: I'm a lawyer now; I got a first from Edinburgh; I moved to Amsterdam. None of the kids who got knocked up at sixteen and live in council flats ever turn up, none of the kids who became addicts or homeless or took a job working as a supermarket cashier make an appearance. Yet those are the ones I want to know about, the ones I think about from time to time. The others, I realise, I don't care about at all, probably never did, the intimacies between us simply part of a performance. I take no pleasure in hearing about positive achievements, even if they are peppered with thankyous. The visits also highlight my inertia. 'Here I am, exactly where you left me, wearing the same smart suit and complaining about the teaching assistants.'

And when the returning student finally leaves, both of us gunked from the awkwardness of an interaction that should have been a shared moment of sentimentality, I might see a current student, an especially troubled one, and be overwhelmed with love, forgetting that, really, I am nothing in that child's life: I am already a part of their history.

•

Jacinta and I both became school teachers. I taught chemistry, she taught art. Then, ten years ago, she called to tell me she was being bullied at work by management. They'd explained that she must find ways for more of her students to get top grades or her job would be at risk. This meant, she knew, doing the work for them. Jacinta was the head of department at an independent school in Winchester and living on site, in rooms owned by the school. With no free time, her life effectively devoted to her wealthy students, she had stopped painting, going to galleries and living her life. At the time my sister had enough expendable cash to wear clothes without labels that rich people would appreciate, but the only rich people who saw her were the students' demanding parents. She said, 'I'm so unhappy, Doughy.'

I'd never heard her talk like that before. Even when she was young and listening to a lot of PJ Harvey.

I said, 'Get another job. Try a state school. I don't know how you cope being around jumped-up little arseholes all day long.'

She sniffed. Or perhaps she snickered. 'I'm not ready for that sort of change,' she whispered.

I had been reading a lot of Anne Lamont so replied very quickly. 'No one is ever ready for change.'

Jacinta left the school a week later, without giving a term's notice, and moved to Brooklyn where she lived with a drag queen and worked in a bar on the Lower East Side. The following year she began an MFA at Columbia. And a few years later she had a solo show in a small Chelsea gallery where her cheapest canvas sold for $8,000.

'Come and see the paintings,' she'd said. 'There's one of Pete.'

'Is there?'

'No. Of course there isn't.'

'Mum's becoming forgetful,' I told her.

'I'm sorry to hear that. Still. Please come and see the show.'

•

My dad died in a housefire six years after he left. It was the summer I turned sixteen. We weren't told much more. And we weren't asked to attend the funeral in Buncrana where his family had a plot ready for each of their children. His girlfriend sent me his leather wallet. It had a fiver in it, plus an expired video shop rental card and a passport photo of a young boy. Jacinta got nothing, so I gave her the wallet and we spent the fiver in McDonalds on cheeseburgers and nuggets.

•

A family of Jehovah's Witnesses moved in next door. The eldest son saw me dancing through our sprinkler in my school uniform, Del Amitri on the radio in the kitchen. He shouted down from his bedroom window: 'You're going to hell.' His hair was shaved so close to his head he looked less like God was his light and salvation, and more like a neo-Nazi.

I took off my shoes and socks. 'Do you want a strawberry Cornetto?'

He hesitated. 'I can't save you,' he said.

His name was Aaron. He had a parakeet and five sisters. We sat with our backs to one another, a splintery fence between us, slurping on the cones until his father showed up and he scurried inside. Pete arrived home from work not long after, he worked for the council, something to do with computers in the social care department, but he was hammered and fell asleep on the sofa in front of Grange Hill. My mum told Jacinta to take off Pete's loafers and put them into the hall with the other shoes. Jacinta refused because she hated the smell of sweaty leather.

We set the table for four but only three of us sat to dinner. Mum said, 'Jacinta, if you don't start practicing your violin, I'm cancelling your lessons.' My sister shrugged. She was sketching in a notebook with a biro. This wasn't allowed at the table when Pete was conscious. Mum said, 'Dolores, elbows.' Gavin was in his third year at university by then. I had my old room back but I slept on Jacinta's floor sometimes. I was nervous being in my own bed.

Aaron's room was next to mine and if I pressed a glass to the wall, I could hear him praying, his tone was steady, tedious.

When he finished, I'd knock: *Rat-a-tat-tat*.
Nothing.

I'd knock again. *Rat-a-tat-tat.* And sometimes he'd reply. *Tat. Tat.* This meant *hi*. It might also have meant, *I want you, Dolores O'Shea. I want you so much. And I love you too.*

•

Del Amitri: 'from the womb.' It is both a very sexy and very not sexy name for a band.

•

I unzipped the bag the whole way so I could see from the crown of her head to her painted toenails. I turned her slightly on to her side and realised, then, she wasn't entirely lifeless. A cable was tucked in under her arm. So she could talk. If charged. She could probably tell me things, if asked. The sex doll in the garage was more than she appeared.

She was also a machine.

A beautiful, intelligent machine.

•

David puts people to sleep for a living. And he is responsible for waking them up again. Asleep. Awake. Alive. Dead. Passive. Inert. Quiet. Crying. Unable to consent. 'Only psychos become anaesthesiologists,' Pierre said.

My praying neighbour, Aaron, jumped in front of a train at Potters Bar station when he was twenty years old. I was back home for the holidays when Mum casually mentioned it. 'Silly lad,' she said. 'He wanted to be a zoo keeper. His poor mother told me. God bless her and save her.' Pete was struggling to open a jar of mayonnaise and groaned.

'Why did he kill himself?' I asked.

Mum frowned as if the question were ignorant. 'He didn't want to be alive,' she said. 'People find it hard to live with themselves sometimes. Maybe he had a secret.'

Pete threw the mayonnaise jar across the room, smashing it against the opposite wall. 'I'm sorry,' he said. 'I don't know why I did that. I'm a bastard.' Mum didn't flinch. She rose from her chair, found a spray bottle and some cloths under the sink, and started to clean.

'You're doing your best,' she told him.

•

I agreed to marry David on one condition: we swap the double duvet for two singles to stop us arguing about who was hot and who was cold every night. I remember him plaiting my hair while we watched the Commonwealth Games on television. I remember he painted my toenails and blew on them to prevent the varnish from sticking to my socks. I remember he came home from a work trip to Belgium with his pockets full of dark chocolate truffles because I was addicted to them. When I looked sad he'd say, 'What's wrong, my sweet?' and more often than not I'd say, 'Nothing,' or minimise my hurt even if something bad had happened. I wanted our lives to be joyful. I didn't want to be the cause of any strife. Sometimes he'd push. 'Tell me, Dolores.' And still. I'd not know how to begin. And David would look discouraged. But not for long.

•

When Jacinta first moved to Brooklyn, she called ridiculously early in the mornings to complain about her problems. She wouldn't respect the time difference. David said, 'I have a real job, unlike Georgia O'Keefe over there.' He liked and respected Jacinta but, even so, he took to sleeping in another room, which frightened me. I told him I'd put my foot down, that Jacinta understood and respected us. The truth was I simply silenced my phone and we didn't hear her cries for help.

It took Jacinta a long time to get to grips with America. The health care system was one of her biggest concerns. She asked me to make appointments for her with various doctors and also speak to the insurance company to find out how much it was going to cost her to have a blood test or be prescribed birth control. She didn't understand how to file her taxes and very quickly owed money to the IRS. She hated their supermarkets and the exorbitant tipping culture. 'Hairdressers expect twenty per cent,' she said. 'You can't get out of a salon without handing over two hundred dollars.'

'Come home,' I told her after a few years. She'd made something of herself and would easily find a gallery to show her work in London.

'No chance,' she said. 'I'd rather eat a wheelbarrow full of fresh shit.'

•

I came across a podcast about a charming self-help guru who convinced his followers to remain inside a makeshift sweat lodge until several of them passed out and three of them died. He fled the scene but many of the followers stayed loyal. He ended up in prison and when released continued to run wellness workshops. He had very white teeth. His wife looked like Olivia Newton-John. He said that pain makes you stronger, that people can harness loss and transform it into power, use it to build a more complete character. But who'd walk into pain willingly? And who stays inside a fucking tent that'll roast you alive?

•

Mum's front door was wide open again. 'Mum?' I called out, closing it. She shuffled out of the kitchen in a pair of large wellies and waved like I was standing at the end of a long pathway. 'Mum?' I said again.

She kept shuffling, a docile zombie, and kissed me on the cheek. She smelled earthy. 'I thought you were Helen,' she said. Her voice was a croak. I assumed I was the first person she'd spoken to that day.

I wanted to say, 'You're too young for all this, Mum.' I said, 'Who's Helen?'

'Margaret?'

'Who's Margaret?'

She pinched her eyebrows trying to remember something and let out a small whine.

'Mum, you shouldn't leave the door wide open. Anyone could come inside.'

She glanced at the closed door and back at me. 'Did you remember the ibuprofen? I have a terrible pain in my neck. I need better pillows. And I should start yoga. You can do it at any age.'

'I can get you some pillows.'

We had tea and digestives and I helped her hang washing on the line. The day was overcast. A magpie perched unsteadily on the fig tree and barked at us. She said, 'How's David? I never see him. Is he busy?'

'He's fine,' I said.

I assumed he was fine.

•

I lay awake wondering whether I should have moved the doll to a different location. This would have forced David to ask me about it. But in the end, I took Jacinta's advice. I changed my security cameras' settings to alert me immediately of any movement along the side of the house, which was the way we usually entered the garage. I couldn't imagine David using the up-and-over doors at the front to access his toy, but even if he did there was a camera there too. I also had one set up at the back of the house and at the end of the garden. He couldn't hide.

•

Ryan Porter was the creator of a cartoon getting passed around Year Ten. In the cartoon, Miss Shannon Coleman, his English teacher, was whipping a boy with a cat-o'-nine-tails whilst he read a copy of *The Mayor of Casterbridge*. His erection was huge, as were her nipples. Ryan was quite the artist. I told him this and then, 'But it's inappropriate, Ryan.'

He was fifteen years old. His mother had died the previous year and his Norwegian father, who he'd only ever seen during the summer holidays, moved from Stavanger to care for him. Ryan's blazer was too big. He kept his hands in his trouser pockets as he slouched in the chair opposite. He was a relentlessly

disruptive student, who I liked more than he deserved.
'It's a laugh though,' he said.

'It's sexual harassment, Ryan. You can't do this sort of thing.'

'Miss Coleman is shagging Oliver Sminton in Year Thirteen. Did you know? That's illegal. I might tell the police. I might go to the station, yeah, and be like, there's a paedo teaching at my school. She's fit, but she's also a paedo.'

I had heard this rumour before and seen Shannon Coleman and Oliver Sminton in the sixth form common room sitting close together, leaning over books like they could be engaged in legitimate learning despite the fact she didn't teach him. Shannon was twenty-four years old with jaunty boobs and a fashionable fringe. Oliver had stubble.

'I don't think that can be true, Ryan. But I'll look into it.' Ryan scanned my office, the various papers taped to the walls, the stacks of files and books on the desk. 'Do you have any work you can get on with until your next lesson?' I asked.

'Did you get your car fixed, Miss?'

'Yes I did.'

He sat up. 'What was wrong with it?'

'A puncture, that's all.'

'Right. Yeah. Well, if it's seen better days, I can arrange to have it stolen for you and written off, for like eighty quid.'

'I'll pretend I didn't hear that,' I said, though I was impressed. 'Can you promise to behave in Miss Coleman's English classes please? Next year I'll arrange to have you taught by Mrs Norman who I know will kick the humour out of you, if you misbehave.'

He snorted. 'Yes, Miss.'

'Promise.'

'Yes, Miss.'

'No more nasty illustrations.'

'No, Miss.'

When he left, and I was alone again in my office with a backlog of emails from disgruntled parents, I had an urge to summon him back. I had an urge to keep Ryan there with me.

He was knowing. He was playful. He was a brave little bastard.

•

As a young teacher I would raise my voice to get a group's attention. Now I know better. To make yourself heard, you get very quiet.

It instils fear.

•

David should have been in theatre, but he wasn't. He was slinking along the side of the house and using a key to unlock the garage door. I watched him step inside and twenty-eight minutes later, I watched him leave and lock the door.

I called him. 'David?'

'What's up?'

'Where are you?'

'I forgot something. I'm at home. I'm leaving in a minute. You alright?'

'What did you forget?'

'Huh?'

'What did you forget? Why are you at home?'

'My iPad.'

'Where had you left it?'

'On the hall table. Has something happened?' Nothing in his voice betrayed his sin. It made my stomach heave.

'I've got parents' meetings after school. Can you sort out dinner?'

'Sure. Shall I pick up some salmon?' he asked.

'I don't know.

'OK. Well, text me.'

'David?'

'I'm rushing, Dolores. Just spit it out for God's sake. What's wrong?'

I put down the phone.

Then I watched a live stream from the front camera: David getting into his car and driving away. I couldn't make out his expression.

•

Gavin crept around at first, when he and Pete moved in. He was five years older than I was and nothing like his father. Better or worse, I cannot say. He kept a bearded dragon in a vivarium in his bedroom and fed it live locusts. He convinced Mum to let us get a kitten. Jacinta called her Longstocking. She got hit by a car a few roads away. The driver didn't even stop. The cremation cost more than the kitten herself. Gavin made Jacinta a sympathy card that she left out in the rain. He bought us sweets sometimes and hid them under our duvets.

•

You only have to look around to know that your problems, however difficult, don't make you special.

•

I am trying to explain.

3

I opened a private window and used my phone data rather than the home Wi-Fi. I clicked on the first recording: a man caressing a doll's face, tucking her long hair behind her ears, admiring her cheerleading costume with its long socks and frills. He complimented her small feet. But then it cut straight to the same man pressing himself into her mouth, his face straining, her eyes impassive. He held her head with two tattooed hands. No noise except his own breath, the odd grunt. Not a squeak from her. He continued. It went on for twelve minutes.

He released the doll's head. Her mouth regained its pout. Her eyes were fixed on nothing. No harm done. No one hurt. She was a mechanism and not real and a machine and had no feelings and was a game and a commodity and a receptacle and an imitation.

I watched another video. Two men. One doll. The fully dressed men took turns to smack the doll. They were sweating from the exertion. The clip lasted for four minutes. Just hitting.

And another video. A straight couple wearing lacy masks to hide their identities.

And another. A man eating his dinner opposite a naked doll.

Another. A man dressed in a black leotard kissing the doll, biting her.

Another. A man rubbing himself between two silicone breasts, the doll lying across a snooker table.

And another. And another. Another another another. The choice was endless.

I was getting wet even though I wanted to use a hammer to smash someone's brains in.

But the men weren't hurting the dolls because dolls can't get hurt. There was a benignity to it. An inconsequence. No one bled. The girls' bodies were synthetic, made of polymers, plastic joints, rubber nipples, hair from acetate. No tearing, crying, bruises, hand-prints, looks of terror towards a camera, no venereal disease or coercive directors.

Disclaimer: No women or children were harmed in the making of those movies.

•

We require trigger warnings.

Do you?

That's funny.

•

Oliver Sminton was loitering outside the staffroom. He held up a notebook. 'Is Miss Coleman in there, please?' I asked if he had an appointment and explained that if she'd had lessons all morning, she'd be busy planning or marking. He waved the notebook again. 'She's helping me prepare for my interview at UCL.'

I congratulated him on this; few students went on to do medicine. 'I'm glad you're preparing, but Miss Coleman is an English specialist. You should have asked one of your science teachers. Or I could help, if you like.' The corridor filled with younger students leaving the library, squealing and tripping over one another. As they knocked past, I took Oliver's elbow and pulled him aside. He stared at the floor, seemed young, though he was over six foot.

'Miss Coleman helped me write my UCAS statement,' he said. His neck reddened as he stood there, bowed with guilt.

'I'll practice with you, and if I'm awful, we could ask my husband to meet you. He's a doctor.' I felt an absurd swell of pride that deflated quickly. 'The interviews for medicine are more gruelling than most. Do you have interviews anywhere else?'

He looked me in the eye at last. 'Birmingham and Cambridge. But I don't want to move too far from the south coast.' He drew back, his thumbnail scratching a rash on his arm. He was a handsome boy, mild and clever. I could see why a young teacher might have fallen for him.

The staffroom door behind me opened.

'Oliver!' Shannon Coleman was wearing a floral dress, opened in a V-shape at the chest. Her nails were manicured, polished in amber to match the flowers in the dress. Not many years before I had taken care of myself this way, perhaps purposely to tempt some of the older students. 'I'll grab my stuff.' I held the staffroom door shut by its handle.

Oliver flinched. He wanted to protect Shannon but couldn't. 'Ms O'Shea said she thinks she should help me because it's a science,' he muttered.

Shannon crossed her arms over her chest. I wondered whether her stomach lurched. 'Oh. Yes. That's a better idea. Naturally!' Was she heartbroken in that moment? Did she ache for the minutes she would not get to spend with this boy?

I didn't want to upset anyone. But I also had a job to do. A duty of care.

I stepped aside and Shannon pushed through into the staffroom and was gone, her honeyed scent lingering. Oliver folded his notebook in half and tried to push it into his back pocket. When it wouldn't fit, he took it in both of his slim hands and twisted it. 'Shall we say lunchtime one day next week?' I asked. 'I'm a bit overwhelmed at the moment.'

He nodded gloomily.

I had made him miserable. I wasn't proud of that.

•

I stopped at the cash machine and took £300 out of the joint account. I stashed it in a baking tin in the microwave. I did this day after day, hundreds then thousands of pounds. David never mentioned it, though he had a banking app on his phone that alerted him every time money was taken from the account.

He also never mentioned the fact I didn't take his surname, when I knew his father was raging about it. And he never said, not once in our whole relationship, 'Why are you the way you are?' It would have been a valid question. And maybe I would have given him an honest answer. I don't know. It's all so easy in retrospect.

•

Twice more I watched David go into the garage when I wasn't at home. I didn't call and compel him to lie. That felt unfair.

On one occasion, as he left the garage, a long forty-three minutes after he first went in, he looked right into the camera's lens and I had the sense he was looking for me. I had the sense he was willing me to catch him.

That was a difficult day.

•

The doll didn't provoke jealousy. Discomfort mostly. And I pitied her – all scrunched up, suffocating in the bag, the idea of David using her then hiding her away like you would a garden fork. He kept his treadmill in the house.

•

Jacinta answered groggily. Ed, her boyfriend, had slept over, and they'd spent the evening arguing about gun control. Ed was not a Republican, but he was an antagonist. Debate seemed to be a thing they did for fun.

'Yes, I'm sure. He's been into the garage three times. And the recording won't disappear for thirty days, so he can't deny it.'

'Good.'

'Is it?'

'No. I'm sorry, Dough.'

•

I stopped at a petrol station to buy flowers for Mum when a woman in a Porsche pulled up next to me. Even before she got out of the car, I could tell she was offbeat: her lips, too large for her face, were like uncooked sausages. As she stepped from the car her full peculiarities were revealed: a spindly body covered from neck to ankle in winding tattoos, breasts larger than footballs and close enough to her own mouth that she could easily have sucked her own nipples.

She was wearing a tank top and mini-skirt. In the passenger seat was a very young man, her boyfriend perhaps, or a son.

I have trained myself not to stare, knowing it's unkind to do so, but this woman seemed to invite attention, her body mostly uncovered, her hair a gigantic platinum shambles wobbling away on her head.

When she caught me looking, I flinched.

She raised her chin in defiance.

But I wasn't disapproving.

I was only looking.

I was interested.

She looked nothing like the doll and surely if you planned to sculpt yourself into a feminine ideal, the doll would be the guideline. Anything more extreme and the transformation tiptoes into self-hatred, self-harm, despair. 'Hey,' I said, 'I like your car.'

The woman touched the shiny, silver roof. 'I bought it myself,' she said.

•

David had started playing tennis a few times a week, was making his way up the club league tables. It was evening. He grabbed his keys from the sideboard. 'You can't go out,' I said. 'We have guests coming for dinner.' This wasn't true. I'm not sure why I said it. Maybe I wanted him to start a quarrel.

He turned. 'Since when? Who?'

I told him I'd invited Gavin and Faye. He pulled his phone from his jacket pocket and started to type. He wasn't cancelling his match. I knew that. He was texting Gavin to postpone a non-existent dinner or to send his apologies for missing the non-existent dinner. He would be honest and explain he had a tennis game. But he would never also admit, *I don't want to see you.* Although he disliked Gavin, David's good manners would never permit complete candour. He had a way of perfectly balancing truth and diplomacy.

Outside, foxes were screeching. And our wheelie bin was full of maggots. I'd noticed earlier that day but hadn't the stomach to deal with them. They were crawling towards the lid. Hundreds, maybe thousands, of them.

'Why is there a sex robot in our garage?'

David's keys clattered against the floor. Then his phone. His eyes searched the hallway for something to aid an explanation. He reached for the wall to steady himself. And then, as if about to give a speech at a conference, he straightened up.

'Her name is Zoey,' he said quietly.

•

Her name is Zoey. That is the first thing he said. Assuredly. Protectively. Her name is Zoey.

A woman said to her spouse, 'Did you hear the one about the wife who asked her husband if he could feel pains across his body as though someone had a voodoo doll of him?'

He said, 'No, why?'

The wife disappeared upstairs then called down to her husband, 'How about now?'

•

David has a switch. I have always envied it, the composure he can access, even in the middle of a crisis. And that's how it was.

'Her name is Zoey,' he said.

I was screaming a reply when the bell rang. 'Don't answer it,' I warned. 'Don't answer that fucking door.'

David seemed about to comply. And then he *did* open the door, taking in a gulp of cold air. Seeing our neighbour he smiled. 'Caleb!' He shook his hand and ushered him inside. 'What's the story?' The switch was on. I'd seen him do this the day his father died. He'd been bawling when the undertakers pulled up outside but stopped as they stepped into the house. David told a preposterous anecdote about his father's childhood, then a quip about death, finally finding money in his wallet for a tip. Should you tip an undertaker? David did. 'Those guys don't earn a lot, Dolores. It seemed the right thing to do,' he'd said.

Caleb coughed into his elbow. 'Oh, you know, misbehaving and trying not to get caught.' He sucked something from his teeth. He'd had his hair cut very short. He was wearing grey slippers.

'Your package.' I retrieved a bulky envelope from the floor. It was the third I'd taken in that week. I was beginning to resent it, especially the food deliveries.

He tapped the envelope. 'CBD oil. Don't tell the cops!'

David laughed and it sounded so clean I thought for a moment I was mistaken, that I would return to the garage and find it empty, or a motorcycle where I thought I'd seen Zoey.

I thought, David isn't worried, so why should I be? My work is stressful, Mum is getting more forgetful, I miss Jacinta. It's me. I have imagined something sordid, like the time I came out of a general anaesthetic and thought I could see a pile of dead chickens in a corner of my hospital room, a fat baby at the centre gorging on them, feathers and all. As I was coming around, I kept asking for Gavin. The nurses asked me who he was and I told them he was my husband.

Caleb said, 'Is it alright if I borrow your sander, guys?'

The tulips on the console table were dying, the water stagnant, stinking. I tapped the vase and some of their pale pink petals landed silently against the table.

I went upstairs and waited for Caleb to leave. I folded the laundry. I cleared my purse of old receipts. Then I heard David's car starting up and pulling away.

•

We went abroad for the first time. A family holiday to France. Mum and Pete sat in the front fretting about driving on the wrong side of the road. Jacinta and I were in the back wishing we were still at home.

Mum had found a cottage in Dieppe on Teletext, called the owner and booked it herself. The place was described as rustic but was actually in disrepair and next door to a bowling alley that flashed neon lights day and night. Pete refused to sleep in any of the damp beds and chose an armchair in the living room. He did this mostly to prove to Mum what a sham foreign holidays were and to sabotage any chance of us going on another one.

A few days after we arrived, Gavin showed up with a girl and a backpack. Her name was Jasmine. She didn't say very much unless it was in fluent French, so we took her with us wherever we went to avoid misunderstandings. On more than one occasion, Pete asked her to query the food bill which she did cheerfully, leading me to think she was simply complimenting the waitress on the food.

Jasmine's arrival invited Pete to cheer up a bit, which he often did with strangers around, and Jasmine was no exception. In fact, he seemed delighted by Jasmine's very existence and kept offering her the best seat, the largest slice of cake. Mum was washing up while he dried the dishes next to her, and I overheard him say, 'Thank God for Jasmine. I was beginning to worry, Geraldine. I was beginning to think...' But he didn't finish his sentence and Mum didn't ask him to explain what he meant.

Gavin and Jasmine slept on a mattress in the attic, and as they ascended a wooden ladder to bed one evening, Jasmine said, 'Your sister's creepy. She won't stop watching me.'

I knew she meant me and not Jacinta who rarely looked up from her sketchbook unless it was to pick a flower for pressing between its pages. I was tempted to shout something up at Jasmine who I didn't like, but the fact I'd overheard her did seem to prove a point.

Gavin said, 'Dolores has had a weird life. It isn't her fault.'

'Yeah, well, it's still creepy.'

They left the next morning, taking a train to Brussels. Jacinta and I went to the beach. All day Jacinta sat in the sun and by the time we got back to the cottage she was bright red. But later, on her thigh, a word began to appear, written in sunscreen with her finger while she'd let the rest of her skin burn: FAUX.

Zoey was manufactured by a company called Love Dolz in a Californian factory by a team of clever software specialists. I found photographs online of the company's headquarters. A blonde doll in a suit sat at a desk and behind her three more dolls dressed in a variety of outfits. All of them had long hair, curves: one was in a sequinned green evening dress, a second in denim shorts and crop top, the third in white lingerie. I was none of those women. I was a woman in wide-leg trousers and expensive slip-ons, my hair to my shoulders, cut bluntly rather than feathered and flirty.

Love Dolz had been producing these toys for ten years, but it was only recently that they'd managed to get the product to move a little and talk. Each piece was completely customisable to the customer. David had been able to choose Zoey's eye colour, nose shape, nipple shape, the size of her tits, arse, the number of freckles on her forearm, the length of her nails, her height.

The sole immutable was her name. Love Dolz had chosen it for all their AI models.

Zoey: life.

You had to hand it to those tech wankers and their sense of irony.

•

David didn't like to kiss open mouthed. It took me a long time to come to terms with this when we were dating. But I did accept it. Just as I accepted a lot of other small things I didn't like. I don't know what he dislikes about me. He's never said.

•

It was my turn to give the lower school assembly, but I had not prepared. I wrote a quick list as children filed into the hall, jacked up on windy weather. The teachers followed the students, pointing and ordering, carrying uncertain loads of exercise books.

Shannon Coleman had a satchel over one shoulder, a handbag over the other. She was clutching a thick paperback. Her hair was tied in a high bun. She wasn't wearing much make-up. She looked perfectly graceful, completely at odds with the scruffy students bumping past her, a few of the boys half-wrestling with one another.

A child stood in front of me. 'Miss, can I go to my trumpet lesson, please?' I couldn't recall the boy's name. He had several badges on the lapel of his blazer: PREFECT, LIBRARIAN, CHAMBER CHOIR. I doubted he had many friends.

'Yes, go on.'

Shannon took a seat at the back of the hall. She scrolled her phone quickly then put it away. Sunlight split the hall in two. She shaded her eyes from the light.

I began:

'Last week a drunk driver collided with a group of local children outside a chip shop in Kemptown and killed a girl. Some of our students knew her. It's a difficult time.

'On Saturday the school's mixed athletics team became district champions after a rocky start to the season. This is an example of how perseverance can prevail. They should all be congratulated.

'Kenza Dunthorne in Year Nine has been given a role in *Matilda* in the West End and leaves us on Friday for several months. We wish her all the luck in the world.

'Students with phones turned on during lessons will have these devices confiscated and returned only to a parent or guardian.'

The children listened in weary silence. The teachers looked equally uninspired, depressed even. But Shannon was beaming, her eyes bright with hope.

•

Zoey is beautiful. It's impossible to pretend otherwise. Especially her mouth. Silently it whispers: *yes please.*

•

Pete was proper English. Mum told people this like it was a confession. She'd say, 'Oh yes, he's grand.

But he's *English*,' mouthing the word like it was the equivalent of calling him a cunt. Jacinta and I had been born in London, at the North Middlesex hospital two years apart, but we knew that, like Mum and Dad, we weren't English. English people didn't serve you a biscuit with your tea when you went to visit, they expected to be phoned up before you called over in case they were busy with private things, and they didn't get a round in at the pub but instead paid for their own drinks as and when they wanted them. They also cried when members of the royal family died because they didn't have a comprehensive understanding of the meaning of democracy.

Our friends at St Joseph's Primary School and later at St Angela's High School were also Irish, unless they were Italian or from one of the Caribbean islands. On prize night half the student body sullenly refused to sing 'God Save The Queen' and everyone sprayed their hair green on St Patrick's Day. Sister Thomas, the headmistress, seemed inclined to do little about any of this, being from Mayo herself.

So when Pete moved in and insisted on baked beans with his fry up and Yorkshire pudding with his Sunday roast, it was a bit of an adjustment, especially for Mum who was initially reassured that, because Pete's dad was from Liverpool, Pete must have had some Irish in him somewhere. But Pete didn't have a dribble of Irish in him and tortured my mother by raising a St George's Cross in the front garden when England played an international game of football, cricket or rugby. If it hadn't been for Ireland's four Eurovision victories in the nineties, which Mum celebrated for months afterwards, buying the CDs and playing them on repeat in the kitchen, I don't think she would have tolerated Pete's brazen Englishness as long as she did.

Gavin was also English, of course. He wasn't proud of it though, and he wasn't a Tory, so somehow it felt less threatening to our way of life.

•

David rang the doorbell before he let himself in. 'It's me!' he called out, loud enough to be heard, meek enough to sound contrite. I stirred the canned chicken soup simmering on the hob. Ignored him. He tipped the kitchen door twice with a knuckle. 'Dolores?' I continued to stir. The soup smelled like dog food. 'I rang the bell,' he said.

'Why?'

His tie was still in place, not loosened to let him breathe at the day's end. 'I booked Moshimo for dinner, if you fancy it.'

'I've got soup.'

David put his hands into his trouser pockets. As he came closer, I turned off the gas and looked for a bowl, just to get away from him. There were no bowls in the cupboard, and I'd forgotten to turn on the dishwasher. I reached for an oversized mug.

'How was work?' he asked.

'Do me a favour, David.'

He unbuttoned his jacket, flicked through the post on the countertop. 'I might go to Moshimo. I'm hungry.'

'OK.'

'Sure you won't come?'

'Are we going to talk about Zoey?' I asked.

He let out a long sigh. 'What do you want me to say?'

'Firstly, those dolls are ten grand. We didn't go away for half-term because things were a bit tight, you said. Ten thousand pounds, David.'

'I know.'

'You *know*?' I put down the mug I was holding to stop myself from flinging it at the wall.

'Actually she was closer to eight thousand.' He went to fridge, looked inside, but finding nothing closed it again.

'David?'

'What?'

'*Why?*'

'I don't know what you want me to tell you.'

'Tell me something. Anything. I don't have a clue what to do with this information about you.'

'What information? It isn't a big deal.'

'What?'

'I don't know how to talk about it,' he said croakily. 'I wanted us to stay together but I didn't want … Jesus, I don't know.' He opened the fridge again, took out a beer and opened it but didn't drink. 'I think I'd rather split up than have to talk about it.'

'You're not being serious,' I said, but I knew he was. He looked and sounded very serious. And I understood. Shame had stoppered him up. He was choking from it.

I wanted to tell him that splitting up wasn't an option, that I needed him and our marriage, and that whatever we had hidden in the folds of our domestic life could be uncovered, explained, repaired.

He said, 'I'll get rid of the doll,' as though Zoey was our problem.

She wasn't.

I was.

It was me he had to get rid of.

•

DNA replicates and duplicates. It is the reason we exist. It answers the question: why am I here?

Why *am* I here?

Because of DNA.

Meaning can be found in biology.

•

David's parents hired a function room for our engagement party. I was marking mock exams when he announced this. I put down my pen. 'I don't want a party. Who's going to come?'

'They're excited. They like you.'

'They want to meet my family.'

'And what's wrong with that?'

'I don't have time to plan a party, David. Ofsted inspectors are in school next month. I'm stressed out. I have nothing nice to wear.'

David smacked my knee lightly. 'Wear something hot.'

'Me?'

'Yes, *you*.'

I had my hair done and wore a blue dress that plunged down the back. On the way to the venue in a taxi, David kept running his thumb down my spine, kept kissing my cheek, forehead, fingers.

On a long table by one wall was an array of elegant finger food and loitering by the bar two servers dressed in black and white. They were holding trays by their sides, waiting for the guests.

David's family were the first to arrive. 'Dolores!' Camille said, opening her arms to me. She smelled as though she'd sprayed herself with several different bottles of perfume. 'Oh, you're an angel. David is so lucky. Isn't he, Ian? Hugo?'

David's brother nodded and his father, who was holding a basket of flowers, deposited the flourish onto the end of the food table. 'Very nice,' Hugo said mildly. He was staring at a waiter.

The guests, most of whom were friends or relations of David's, drifted in and were met at the door by a tray of fizzing champagne flutes. The music was loud enough to keep things from feeling too uncomfortable. The food was replenished when platters began to empty.

Leonard arrived with a woman I'd never met and told me he couldn't stay long, that he had a book launch the same evening. 'Was I meant to get you guys a present? I don't know the etiquette.'

He began to introduce me to the woman at his side, a German publisher, when Mum, Pete and Gavin tumbled into the room. Mum was wearing a floral dress with a bright yellow bolero, Pete was in a velvet blazer and Gavin had worn cargo trousers and a pink shirt. It had started to pour moments earlier, and the dash from the car park to the pub had soaked all three of them. No one except me had turned to look, but they seemed at that moment to have a spotlight shining on them. They were so bedraggled, colourful, and out of keeping with the energy in the room. Mum spotted me and marched over, her sling-backs loud and angry.

'You didn't say it would take over an hour to get here. We were killed in the traffic.'

'That's OK. You're here,' I said.

Pete and Gavin grabbed glasses of champagne and joined us. Pete said, 'You'll catch your death in that dress'

Gavin looked around the room and not directly at me. Then he said, 'Are those the in-laws?' He had correctly identified Ian and Camille, who were animatedly chatting with a couple I'd never seen before.

'She's not a bad looking woman,' Mum said.

Pete downed half his glass. 'Where's Jacinta?'

'She isn't well. Some tonsil thing.'

'I wasn't told,' Mum said.

Jacinta had called as soon as I sent the invitation begging to be excused. 'I'll hate it. I'll end up throwing handfuls of cake at someone. You know what I'm like.' I didn't believe Jacinta would misbehave in any way, but I happily liberated her from the obligation, and in exchange she sent me a thank you card with a joint taped into it.

David joined us with his parents and introductions were made, everyone smiling, well-mannered. Camille told a story about how David, as a boy, told them he would never get married because he wanted to be a troll and live beneath a bridge so he could scare goats. It was a sweet anecdote, one any parent might tell for a gentle laugh, but I could see Mum's mouth begin to tighten, her defenses rising. 'You haven't a glass of anything,' Camille noticed, tapping Mum's hand. She called over a waiter. Mum accepted the drink and took a stiff sip.

The chatting continued, led by Ian and Camille, and I felt my shoulders release until I noticed Ian staring at something. He was squinting slightly and maybe grinning. I followed his gaze and landed on Pete's sleeve, on the little label that had been sewn onto the cuff of his blazer, a label that should have been snipped off, but which Pete clearly thought was an indication of the item's worth, and left there for all to see.

My knees buckled slightly. I leaned against David. David whispered, 'You OK?'

'I'm good,' I said. But I wasn't. I was mortified by my family who couldn't conform to any ordinary social situation, and I was nauseated by David's parents pretending to be the fucking Waltons. I hadn't asked for this party, and here was Ian looking down on Pete who had driven from London, loved my mother, given her a second chance in life, and wasn't perfect, wasn't interesting, wasn't much of anything, but didn't deserve to be sneered at, even internally, by a person who didn't even sleep in the same room as his wife.

Interrupting whatever was then being discussed, I took Pete by the elbow and led him away from the group. 'What's happened?' he asked. 'What's going on?'

'You're not to drink. You have to drive home.'

'Don't worry about that. Gavin's driving. He's only having one.' Pete tilted his head to look at me then, and put a hand on my shoulder. 'It's a lovely party, Dolores. Thanks for asking us.'

I turned around to look at the room of people. I wanted Jacinta there, someone who would understand the delicate nature of my role. I caught Leonard's eye and he pointed at his watch. 'I'd better go and chat to him,' I said, and without asking Pete's permission, put my finger and thumb beneath the label on his sleeve, and ripped it off the blazer.

'You don't need that, Pete,' I said.

'Oh,' he replied. 'Oh. I didn't know.'

•

I met Oliver Sminton in the sixth form common room. He was slouched in a low chair tapping his phone. 'Busy working, Mr Sminton?'

He sat up, turned the phone so I could see the screen. 'I'm learning Mandarin.'

'Why?'

'Even if I get into medicine, I might do something else afterwards,' he said. He stood and put the phone into his backpack. The only reason he hadn't been chosen as head boy was that he'd specifically asked not to have his name on the ballot – he wanted to focus on other things, he'd said to his head of year when she told him he'd made the shortlist.

'Do you speak any other languages?' I asked.

'Spanish. A bit of French.'

The common room smelled of burnt toast and bleach. Each of the dozen or so students was staring into a phone, even those at desks with books arranged around them. 'Might I remind you all that gaps in your timetables are called study periods. Think about the other seventeen- and eighteen-year-olds around the country fighting for the place at university you claim you want.' The students stopped chattering and delved into their lockers for books and photocopied bits of paper.

Oliver said, 'Thank you for taking the time to help, Miss.' He chewed his lips but didn't break eye contact. I wondered whether he was flirting with me, whether the rumours about Shannon and Oliver were simply the result of the way Oliver interacted with everyone.

'Actually, I can't help you today, Oliver. Something urgent has come up.'

'OK.'

'I'll find you another time.'

'Shall I ask Miss Coleman?'

'No. No, don't do that.'

•

David and I took a trip to Kauai for our honey-moon. The first evening, while he was having a bath, I watched a film with Goldie Hawn and Kurt Russell about a wealthy woman who loses her memory and unwittingly falls for a pig of a man with a dirty house and too many children. David had left the bathroom door ajar, warned me jokingly about his nudity. The hotel was all inclusive; I told him it was sushi night and suggested we shake a leg. I hoped lobster would also be on the menu and didn't want to miss out. I could hear David grumbling then he used his foot to push the door closed. He was so long in the water it must have gone cold.

At dinner he told me he wanted to find a driving range. I said, 'Of course!' but he was sullen. The next morning while he hit balls into the abyss, I read a battered copy of *Wide Sargasso Sea*.

Later we drove to the the Kuilau Ridge trail. I'd read the guidebook. It was an easy hike, relatively short. No need for a permit.

The trail was wet from rain that morning but even so we came across local families picnicking and plenty of other walkers. David saluted them encouragingly. He made a lone woman walker blush.

By the time we saw the peak of the Makaleha Mountains it was noon. The air was gluey. I drained my water bottle which had only been a quarter full at the outset. David gulped down water from his own bottle. 'Do you have a spare hat?' I asked.

'Just the one I'm wearing.' He put his cap onto my head.

'No, you need it.'

He didn't reply. He took a photo of us with the mountain in the background. 'Shall we head back and go for a swim?'

Half an hour later I was lightheaded, slipping on mud and wishing I'd worn something more sensible than a pair of Crocs.

David gave me his water bottle. 'Keep it,' he said. He was hiking ahead of me. The backs of his knees were sweating.

'What about you?' I asked him.

He kept walking, holding his hands out in front of him, presumably in case he fell. I swigged from his water. And five minutes later another swig, unable to ration it. By the time we got back to the trailhead, David's eyes were puffy, his hatless forehead burnt.

'I didn't understand the whole shaved ice thing until now,' he said. 'I'd kill for one.'

In the car I put on the air-con and radio.

That night, instead of having sex, we made love. Maybe for the first time. Maybe for the last time. Everything was soft and slow, and I was there in the bed not watching myself from the other side of the room going through the motions and rating my performance. David made eye contact. He told me he loved me. I wanted that to be the way we always were. But we weren't like that.

We were whip-smart and busy. We were successful and nice to one another. We talked and talked and talked about politics and plans for retirement and the psychological problems we encountered in other people. We talked and talked and talked about nothing.

It was a Saturday, torrential rain. Mum called and said she thought there was water coming into her kitchen, but she couldn't be sure, it could also be a radiator leak. I went over to check, stopping quickly at Marks and Spencer for scones. Mum was annoyed that I'd bought clotted cream rather than double cream for whipping and said she preferred blackcurrant to strawberry jam. 'Next time I won't bring anything. I won't even come,' I said, using a wad of kitchen towel to soak up a small puddle on the floor in the living room. Mum had left a soaking towel over the radiator which had simply dripped onto the floor. 'I'll make a pot of tea,' I said.

Mum called out from the sitting room. 'Use the teapot with the chipped lid. The other one dribbles.'

When I went back in with the tray, she was using her cardigan cuff to clean the glass of a framed photo of Pete. It was a picture taken months before he died, at Faye's birthday party. 'That's a good photograph of him,' I said.

'I miss him,' she said.

'I know, Mum. Me too.'

'Bollocks,' she said. She was right. Pete wasn't someone I ever attached myself to. I felt very little of his loss when he died. But Mum loved him, and I felt that. 'I hated keeping things from him.'

'What did you keep from him?' I asked.

She put the frame back onto the side table. 'Makes me angry.' Her voice was sharp and mean, a voice I knew well, a voice she saved especially for me and Jacinta.

I handed her a cup of tea and began to prepare a scone. 'What do you want with yours?' I asked.

'However it comes,' she said through clenched teeth.

It was the dementia taking a grip, I told myself. She couldn't help it. Her brain wasn't her own. I told myself a lot of things hoping they were true. I buttered her a scone. 'No jam then?' I asked.

'Yes, please. Jam, please,' she said.

•

It seemed like every time Jacinta and I visited Faye and Gavin, Faye was sunning herself and Gavin was building Lego. This was when they first got together and moved into a slummy cottage in Granchester. They'd decided to be writers, so it seemed a fitting location. I asked Faye what she was working on. She was lying in the middle of the garden, on a lawn swarming with dandelions and daisies. She removed her sunglasses and turned onto her side. 'It's a literary sci-fi. A girl tries building her own rocket so she can go into space. She isn't an engineer and enlists the help of a local recluse to help.'

Gavin brought out lemonades and left them on the patio. They didn't have any furniture.

'Is it a romance?' Jacinta asked. 'It sounds like you've plotted it with the intention of the protagonist falling in love with the recluse.'

Faye shook her head. She had long red curls that landed lightly between her shoulder blades. Her skin had a blue hue. 'Romance is not a word I'd want associated with my writing.'

'Whether you'd want it associated with your writing or not is irrelevant,' Jacinta continued. She reached for a lemonade, drank a mouthful then promptly spat it back into the glass. 'That's very bitter.'

Gavin stood between Faye and Jacinta like some sort of cultural referee. 'It's a literary exploration of boundaries, wouldn't you say, babe?' he said.

Faye rolled onto her back. The sun had hidden behind a cloud. 'Gavin's poetry is razor-edged. You should read some for them, darling.'

Mum and Pete were in Camber Sands, only the two of them on holiday for the first time ever, and we'd been instructed to use one of our free weekend days to take a trip to see Gavin and Faye, the other to clean the bathroom.

'I don't like poetry,' Jacinta said. 'I prefer mysteries. Maybe one of you should write a detective novel. I borrow tapes from the library and listen to them when I'm painting.'

Faye found a tube of sunscreen next to her on the lawn and squirted some into her hand. I watched as she applied it to her legs, starting at the thigh and moving down to her feet in long hooping strokes.

'I've got quiche for lunch,' Gavin said.

'What type?' Jacinta asked. She was watching Faye too, with a look of deep disgust.

'Lorraine.'

'Good.'

I helped Gavin in the kitchen while Jacinta planted the lavender we'd brought as a gift and Faye continued to lie in the sun. I chopped the tomatoes and cucumbers for the salad, washed the lettuce. Once or twice I almost nicked my fingers with the knife. My body felt clumsy and tight.

Gavin was very quiet, unboxing the readymade quiche and putting it into the oven, washing up four plates and enough cutlery for all of us.

'Jacinta likes ketchup with her food,' I reminded him.

'I have some of that but the lid might be a bit gunky.' He reached over me to retrieve it from a high cupboard and his whole body was against me. He handed me the bottle. 'How's school?' he asked.

'Fine.'

'You're clever, Dolores. Don't waste it, yeah? Make sure you do your best. Get as far away from those fuckers as possible.' He put an arm around my shoulder and squeezed. 'I love you, you know.'

'I know,' I said.

I began to feel annoyed about anything requiring a charge. I started to hate the laptop David had bought me the previous year, my Bluetooth headphones, the lawnmower. Jacinta liked to FaceTime but even that reminded me of Zoey and David and the videos of the dolls with stretchy mouths. I sent some letters in place of emails. Leonard said, 'You've lost your mind, I think, sweetie. Sweetie, have you lost your mind?'

I had. But I said, 'No. Isn't it fun to get a letter?'

'It's fun to know your friend isn't going to end up on the news because she's taken a machete to a crowd of strangers in the Waitrose dairy aisle.'

'I'm full of violence,' I admitted.

'David still not speaking?'

'Is he saying anything to you?'

'He told me he feels ashamed and asked who you'd told.'

'What did you say?'

'I told him that apart from the billboard at Kings Cross Station, you'd said nothing to anyone else.'

'I wonder how much it would cost to do that.'

'Please, Dolores, put the machete away.'

•

David was home early, sitting at the dining table logged in to some international medical conference.

He waved at me not to go, so I made myself a cheese and ham sandwich and sat at the opposite end of the table.

He contributed evenly every so often to what I assumed was a panel event, and his comments were met with approval and deferential questions. He was dressed smartly and shaved, but beneath the table he was in his sports socks.

The conference came to an end and he closed his laptop. 'That ran over by twenty minutes.'

'You should have clicked out. Blamed the broadband.'

He laughed. 'If Covid taught us nothing else, it was to blame the internet.'

'Have you had dinner?' I asked.

'I have tennis tonight. I'll eat afterwards.'

I pushed my plate towards him, half a sandwich still on it. 'Have that.'

'I don't want it.'

'OK.'

'How was your day?' he asked.

'Same as most days.'

'How's your mum?'

'A pain in my arse.'

He laughed. 'We should get tickets for the Rothko exhibition and take her. I think it finishes soon.'

'Where is it?'

'The Tate Modern? I can't remember.'

'Right.'

David was still so handsome, maybe more handsome than he'd been as a younger man. He had gentle eyes.

'Oh, and I was talking to Hugo yesterday. He told me he was planning a big thing for Mum's birthday next month. We should probably contribute something.'

'What?'

'Five hundred quid?'

I shrugged.

'Is five hundred too much?' he asked.

'David.'

'Yeah?'

'Tell me what you're thinking.'

'You wouldn't want to know what I'm thinking.'

'I would.'

'I'm thinking this feels fantastic.'

'Stop it.'

'I know what you're trying to do though. It happened the day we met. You're going to get me to talk. Then you can listen and sympathise and forgive me so we can be what we've always been. But I want you to punch me. Be angry. For once, Dolores. Have a back bone.'

'For God's sake, David.'

'Don't.'

'Don't what?'

'Don't say whatever bullshit you're going to say to smooth all this over because I'll get up and go.'

So I didn't say another word. Neither of us did. We sat staring into the table. And eventually David stood up and left. That's the thing: he left anyway.

•

It's true. We never really argued. We weren't any good at it although we came close a few times. Like when Mum and Pete celebrated their fifteenth anniversary and David told me it was an excuse for gifts and a party because they weren't even married. 'Why can't they have gifts and a party if they want gifts and a party?' I asked. We were in the car on the way to their house. I had a bottle of wine with me and a framed photograph of Mum and Pete from the year they met. Mum had called twice that morning asking whether people would expect servers. I told her no because I knew that by 'people' she meant David.

'I'm not saying they shouldn't do what they want. But people force everyone around them into celebrating minor milestones. Like gender reveal parties for pregnant couples. I mean what the hell is that about?'

'That's different.'

'Is it?'

'We had an engagement party. And a wedding.'

'I know.' He looked in the rearview mirror and frowned. The driver behind us was getting very close.

'Would you rather be somewhere else today?' I asked.

'Yes.'

'Where?'

'Anywhere.'

I felt a jolt of upset but I said, 'Me too.'

David tightened his grip on the steering wheel. 'Who's going to be there?'

'Family mostly. Oh, come on, I tolerate your lot,' I said.

'You *tolerate* them?'

'I didn't mean it like that. You know I didn't.'

David put on his indicator and, with a jolt, pulled into a layby to allow the driver behind us to pass. I thought he might cut the engine so we could continue our discussion, but as soon as the road was clear he pulled out again. 'You don't like my family?' he asked.

'I do,' I told him. And I did. There was nothing to particularly dislike. They were very tepid people.

'OK.' And in a softer voice he said, 'We should have got your mum a better gift. Let's buy some John Lewis vouchers next week and send them.'

'What we got is enough.'

'Are you sure?'

'Yeah.'

'OK.'

And that was it. We got close. Quite close to saying something reckless and then retreated.

Jordana Kenton's mother was ten minutes late and didn't apologise for it. As I led her into my office she said, 'I tried making an appointment with you last week when it happened.'

'I'm glad you've made time this week to see me, Mrs Kenton. And it's nice to meet you in person.'

She sat without being asked, placed a garish handbag on the chair next to her. Her tracksuit was made of cashmere. I took my seat behind the desk. 'So.'

'Well, like I said in my email, I'm not happy about Mr Barry's behaviour. He's made Jordana cry twice in his lessons. The first time it was because she'd not fulfiled the brief, so *he* said. He wouldn't let her show her presentation even though he showed everyone else's. And a couple of weeks ago he shouted at her for handing out party invitations. He then said, and I'm quoting him here because I heard it not only from Jordana but from her friend too, *You might not make it to your twelfth birthday, so hold off on the excitement for a while.*' Jordana's mother wore a tight ponytail that pulled back the skin around her eyes. Her nails were pointy. She was in the Nothing-To-Fucking-Do-All-Day parent category which accounted for approximately half my workload.

I leaned towards her. 'Do you think there's any chance Mr Barry was being humorous?'

Jordana's mother stretched her neck, her left ear to her left shoulder then her right ear to the right. I examined the shine of her engagement ring, and thought how difficult it must be to maintain such pristine standards with regard to one's appearance. I wondered whether it was a strain, the process of becoming the woman she emerged as each day.

'Is he qualified?'

'Who?'

'Mr Barry.'

'Yes. All our teachers are qualified.'

'As what? Comedians?'

Jordana hadn't inherited her mother's wit. Mrs Kenton used the tapered end of the nail on her index finger to scratch at the wooden arm of the chair she was sitting in.

'Jordana has been late probably a dozen times this year. Is there a reason for it?'

As Mrs Kenton replied, explaining how many children she had and the route she took to drop each of them to their respective schools, I wondered what David was doing with his afternoon. Saving a life, perhaps. Being formidable. I'd turned off the camera notifications so he might also have been at home with Zoey.

'Do you think there's an argument to be made for Jordana getting herself to school? On a bus for example.'

'She's eleven.'

'Soon to be twelve. Most of our Year Sevens don't get dropped off by their parents.'

'A fourteen-year-old girl was dragged into a car park off Old Shoreham Road last week. Did you hear about that?'

'I did hear about that, yes. We've suggested students come to school in pairs for a while. Buddy-up.'

'Are we going to talk about Mr Barry? That's why I'm here.'

'Of course,' I said. 'Let me talk to Mr Barry and see how this can be resolved.'

She nodded. But I had no intention of saying a word about any of it to Thomas Barry who was one of our best, most popular teachers. I planned to talk to Jordana and explain that grassing up every teacher who said something she didn't like wasn't going to get her very far at all.

•

My mum's sister Kitty visited from Malahide with her baby, my cousin Paulie, when he was three months old. Kitty's husband was a labourer on the Queen Elizabeth II bridge over in Dartford and was rarely home to Ireland to see them, so Mum told Kitty to stay with us, that we'd help for a while. Pete wasn't happy, being part of the chorus instead of centre stage, but Mum mostly ignored his sulks and spent long hours showing Kitty how to sooth Paulie and when to let him cry. Kitty spent a lot of time in the garden smoking and listening to Richard Marx on Pete's new portable CD player. When Mum started to look really tired, my aunt offered to take Jacinta and me swimming, though once there Kitty disappeared, telling us that if we told no one she'd left us alone, we'd get Slush Puppies on her return. She even had us take her one piece into the pool so it would smell of chlorine. We told no one about Kitty's absconding, and never properly discussed it between ourselves either because freedom like that was rare, as were the Slush Puppies.

Then Kitty went from sleeping in Jacinta's bed, Jacinta pressed up next to me, to sleeping on the sofa. Kitty said the mattress was thin and uncomfortable, but I guessed she just wanted some respite from Paulie who stayed in our room, in a travel cot wedged between our beds. It meant we couldn't be noisy after seven in the evening or put on a light to read. Mum said, 'We all need our sleep, and if he's not let rest, none of us will be.'

'Why can't he be with Gavin? They're both boys,' Jacinta said.

'That doesn't mean much,' I argued. I didn't want Paulie to be with anyone else. I liked his gurgles and the yoghurty smell of our room when he'd been sleeping in it. Mum left bottles of formula on the chest of drawers for when he woke at night and the job of his feeds migrated to us.

Paulie would wake and make a sound so shocking to my system, I'd bolt upright immediately. Then I'd grab him, so no one else would be disturbed, find the formula and take him into bed with me. His fuzzy head was so tiny I could have crushed it between my fingers. I thought how easy it would have been to break an arm or leg, how effortless his murder would have been, how risky it was to pair a strong person with a weak person.

For the last few weeks of their visit, I pretended Paulie was my own baby. I'd walk him, grinning at strangers who peered into the pram with reproachful grimaces. To them I was little more than a tart. And even that fantasy stirred something in me, the idea of being seen in that way, as something menacing and fleshy.

When Kitty and Paulie eventually flew back to Ireland, Pete cheerfully offering to drop them to Stansted and Mum sending them off with some flapjacks Gavin had baked the night before, I sobbed. I missed the weight of my cousin against me, his guileless screams for milk and affection. The cot was removed from our room and there was space to move around again. Jacinta began skipping with a rope all knotted and frayed. But fret filled that space too. And so I kept the lights on whether we were reading or not. For a long time.

A handwritten sign appeared on the staffroom notice board: *Are they attention seeking or connection seeking?*

I considered ripping it down but couldn't find a moment when the staffroom was empty. It stayed up there a long time, until someone else removed it.

•

I have a photograph from my wedding day on the desk in my office. Out of every picture, it is my favourite, taken at the end of the evening when David and I were saying our goodbyes. I am crouching to hug a ten-year-old Paulie in his short-sleeved shirt. He is beaming as he holds me. His eyes are scrunched closed. He is holding on and holding on. It is pure love.

•

A few years into the marriage David asked me to talk to him while we had sex. We were usually silent, not even a low moan. 'Say something,' he whispered. Then, 'Say *something*.'

'What do you want me to say?'

'I don't care. Tell me the best way to gut a goose. I want to hear your voice.'

We'd moved to Acton, bought roller blinds for all the rooms even though it was a rental. 'Shh,' I said, unable to focus, unable to sustain my arousal while he yabbered on. 'Please.'

•

Connection: a relationship in which a person or thing is linked or associated with something else.

•

David couldn't fit everything into one suitcase and resorted to stuffing belts and trainers into carrier bags. I sat on the end of the bed and watched him. I had an urge to remove each item he put into the bags. I had an urge to shake him. I had an urge to fall onto my knees and ask what it was he needed me to be. I said, 'I'm not sure why we're splitting up.'

He had been crying. He didn't look at me. 'What do you want me to say?' he asked. 'Can you pass me that shirt?'

'I want to understand,' I told him.

He shook his head. 'No, you don't.'

'How do you know what I want?'

'If I told you what it's like to be in love with you, it would hurt you to hear it, Dolores.'

'We haven't even tried.'

He stopped for a moment and looked at me sadly. 'I have tried. For years. For ever.'

'We could talk to someone. Work things out.'

'You talk to someone. I think you should. But I can't help with that. I'm not blaming you. I know I'm difficult too.'

'I'm difficult?' I said.

His sweater was creased. His hair was stuck up at the back like he'd slept on it. 'I'll call you.'

'Where will you go?' I asked.

He looked at me like I was a child who needed to be told an adult truth and said, 'Shall I take Zoey with me now or is it OK if I come back for her?'

•

At my Aunty Kitty's funeral three years ago, after lowering her coffin into the ground with his father and our uncles Eamon and Shaun, Paulie held up the bar. He chortled with friends and drank pint after pint of stout. By late afternoon, he could hardly stand up. His jacket looked tailored against his slim build. He had large teeth that made him look like a boy still growing into his own face. His short beard made him seem wise. His eyeliner had smudged.

In the church and then at the reception he never acknowledged me, despite the trips he and Aunt Kitty continued to take to England as he grew up, all the times I'd driven him to the cinema and to Burger King and to Paperchase where I allowed him to pick out whatever he liked.

Before I left, I touched his shoulder, felt the heat from his body. He turned. 'Paulie, I wanted to say I'm so sorry.' He nodded. 'And I wanted you to know that when you were a little boy, I cared about you so much. Do you remember that?' I didn't tell him that I still cared about him. That I loved him. It seemed true but it could have been the occasion that made me feel what I was feeling for him and later read like melodrama.

His nostrils flared a little. He looked ready for a fist fight. He was wearing a gold signet ring on his middle finger. The friend next to him excused himself and we were alone.

I wanted to put my arms around Paulie, smell his neck, remember the baby he had been and the mother I had wanted to be, know the man he was becoming and the woman I'd become. 'I remember,' he said. I took my hand from his shoulder.

Even that had been too much.

·

The night David left, I wrapped myself in a blanket and drank ouzo, the only booze I had in the house. How had everything turned to shit when I'd only ever done the right thing? I was easygoing and easy with forgiveness. I wasn't a cheat or a thief or a liar. Usually. And yet I was alone.

No. I wasn't even alone: my husband's sex doll was still in the garage, stuffed into that bag like a dead whore.

And I thought about them alternately: David, Zoey, David, Zoey. Until I went to sleep.

•

I don't love you anymore, Dolores. I'm not in love with you, Dolores. I never loved you, Dolores. I don't know how I feel about you, Dolores. I don't love you, Dolores. I don't think you love me, Dolores. I don't feel you're in love with me anymore, Dolores. You never touch me, Dolores. You've never loved me, Dolores.

Is this what he'd meant when he said he found me difficult?

4

The still waters of our relationship, the peace David had brought to my life, they were gone. We had dated without zeal, felt no heat in our married life. But without him an ache did open up. Pain loomed. And a kind of haunting, like living with the story of what should have been if only I'd had my eyes open.

•

I left Zoey in the bag until I got into the house, so the neighbours wouldn't see her. She was heavy. The straps dug in to my shoulder, and I ended up dropping her in the kitchen and dragging the bag into the living room. I sat, put my hands into in my lap, my feet together, like I was in a waiting room. The bag was lacy with spiderwebs. My heart was in my neck.

I got up and shut the blind, checked my phone for missed calls or messages. I thought having Zoey laid out flat in my house might untangle the knots in my head, but I was hot and tired.

I sat cross-legged on the carpet and unzipped the bag, not a little, not taking a guilty peek, but unwrapping the whole body from head to toe, giving her space to move and breathe.

Zoey's vest had ridden up. I could see her belly button, evidence of nothing really, but I was embarrassed for her. Gently I put a finger to it and into it, the shallow hollow in her narrow tummy. Then I drew my index finger along the length of her middle, from the band of her leggings to just under her breasts, gathering up the fabric of the vest as I touched her.

I zigzagged my fingers down her arm to her fingers, finding each of her tiny freckles on my way down, like join the dots. Her skin was soft, hairless, not human, but very close.

In the bag the charging cable was wound around itself. I took it out and plugged it into the wall socket then knelt next to the body, feeling around for an inlet which I found at the top of where her spine should have been, hidden beneath her glorious hair. I plugged her in and sat. I sat for a while and when nothing happened, I went into the kitchen and put on the kettle.

•

Leonard phoned. 'I'm in Cheltenham for some book events,' he said. 'I wanted to make sure you were OK.'

'Where's David?' I asked. 'He wouldn't tell me where he was going. He took his passport with him.'

'He's still in the UK. He's staying with his brother for a while.'

'And then what's he doing?'

'He wouldn't say any more. Not to me anyway.'

'I didn't do anything wrong, Leonard. I asked him to talk to me.'

'Maybe he'll come over later.'

'He won't.'

'OK. If he doesn't, I'll call him tomorrow. See what he's thinking.'

'I won't ask you to choose between us, Leonard.'

'I choose you, Dolores,' he said. 'I mean, what the actual fuck was he thinking you'd do when you found out? Did he think you'd pretend you hadn't even seen it?'

•

Yes. Yes, I think David thought I would ignore Zoey if I found her. I mean, I had ignored everything else: his late nights and addiction to sport, his reticence and his sadness and his loneliness and his despair.

•

I let Zoey charge overnight, and when I came down the next day the light on the power adapter was solid green. I unplugged her and using the small switch beneath the slot in her neck, switched her on. Still, she was lifeless. I lay a hand flat against her thigh and squeezed. It gave a little. I squeezed harder expecting her to yip. But nothing existed in her limbs to tell her computer to respond. I could have kicked her with full force and she would have remained silent.

So I texted Leonard.

He replied: *She must be back to factory settings. Download the app.*

The app: Love Dolz.

•

I called Gavin and told him what had happened. 'You've got to be joking.'

'I'm not joking.'

'What did he say? I don't get it.'

'He isn't saying much.'

In the background I could hear either Maya or Freddie screaming. I hadn't seen them in about six months. When Jacinta moved away David and I went to see them a lot less. This was partly David's fault. He resented spending his weekends with Gavin's family when he could have been doing his own thing. 'He isn't your brother,' he'd say. And I think Faye felt the same way about me. It was jealousy, I suppose, in a way. And intuition: the brain sees two or more incongruous details and a narrative in the subconscious cannot be established.

'Do you want me to speak to him?' Gavin asked.

'I'm not sure that would make any difference.'

'I'm a man. It might.'

'Leonard tried.'

'Leonard's gay. It isn't the same thing.'

'I don't think so.' Another scream in the background made me pull the phone away from my ear. 'Everything alright?'

'I have to go, sib,' he said. We'd taken to calling one another sib in the last ten years or so. It was something else that annoyed our spouses. 'Why don't you come over for lunch next weekend? Sorry. Sorry. I *have* to go. I'm getting the eyes.' He laughed at Faye's control, or at his own willingness to be controlled, or at me. I don't know.

•

The sea was still, the coast dotted with paddle boarders. The Rampion wind turbines didn't rotate for days. I went to the beach in the evenings, sat on the stones and envied the swimmers' courage. I brought boiled eggs I'd prepared that morning so I wouldn't be tempted to stop at Marrocco's for ice cream. I peeled them carefully, storing the shell in a napkin. I searched for beautiful stones, ones I couldn't return to the crowd, turning their smoothness over in my hands as the turbines watched, motionless. But the stones were useless once I possessed them. Especially the small ones. They ended up on the hall table or in a pocket. They became forgotten things.

•

I called David and he picked up before I heard it ring. 'Hi,' he said. I could tell he'd been awake for a while.

'I haven't heard from you in days,' I said.

He paused. 'I'm trying to give you space to adjust.'

'And get some space?'

'I suppose so.'

'You can come home. You don't have to stay with Hugo. This is your house.'

'I don't want to come home,' he said. 'And I don't think you want me to either.'

I wasn't sure. I didn't miss him exactly, but I missed something. His body-warmth around the house, the ways we moved without bumping up against one another. The sound of his key in the door.

'I hope you're alright,' I said.

'I'm not. But I will be,' he said.

•

Leonard booked a tapas place off Wardour Street and was already halfway through a bottle of wine when I arrived. 'I got us red,' he said.

He didn't stand to greet me but did close the newspaper he was reading and take off his glasses. 'You need new jeans. Those don't fit,' he said. I sat down and he poured me wine, a measure so large it could be considered uncouth. Then he refilled his own glass and ordered a second bottle. 'So, David's a weirdo. Who'd have guessed it?'

'You didn't.'

'I always thought he was gay.'

'No, you didn't.'

'I always hoped he was gay.'

The waitress wandered over with the wine and tried to take our food order but was quickly waved away. His hair was darker than I remembered. I wondered whether he'd been dyeing it.

'How's Pat?' I asked.

'Pat? Oh, Pat. No. He was a little hysterical.'

'Your children's authors usually are.'

'He's an illustrator too, so under some illusion that he's sort of cool.'

'Oh.'

'Shall we have some Padrón peppers to get us started?'

'I'll try some.'

Leonard held out a hand. 'I know you feel like crap, so I won't wisecrack for at least the next hour. I want to hear about it.'

'It's humiliating.'

'For who?'

His skin was rough and I found myself offering him olive oil from the table to soften it. He ordered the peppers, some octopus and meatballs, and I asked if he had any new books to send me. He'd moved from one publishing house to another until setting up his own literary agency. 'Nothing good,' he said. 'The trash I represent, honestly. Celebrities and chefs. That's where the money is, but not the sexy prose, sadly. Having said that, I have recently taken on a literary author who looks like a young Elton John, so that's fun. I try to get song lyrics into our emails.'

'Don't shag him.'

Leonard shrugged as if he might, or might not, but couldn't promise anything. He was still unmarried and by then an orphan. I decided I needed to call him more often, be a better friend, like the one I'd been to him before I married David.

He asked what the worst thing about it was and I had to admit I didn't know. It might have been the secret, or the money, or his being a doctor, but what I knew for sure was that it wasn't the fact that David had probably discharged himself into one of Zoey's holes.

'Are they tight?' Leonard asked. I was about to taste a meatball but put down my fork. I thought of Zoey, her fair skin and guiltless, big eyes. 'Oh, come on. That shock has to be performative.' He spoke with his mouth full. 'If she was in my house, I'd have fingered her by now. Just to feel what it was like. That's what I'd do. And maybe more,' he said.

Zoey was still in the living room, sitting on the sofa staring into the wall. And for no good reason, thinking of her all alone, bored and ignored, made me so sad I couldn't eat another thing.

·

The Love Dolz app was free, presumably because Zoey herself was a shaft. The first thing I had to do was type in my name and pronoun:

David/he

On the screen a photo of a doll much like Zoey appeared. Beneath it, text: *Hi, David! I'm Zoey. I'm trying to find you. Make sure you're close to me so we can make a connection.*

I waved my phone next to her head. Her lashes stirred. And a message popped up:

Hi, David! We're all set. Once you've tweaked my personality here in the settings, you can put away your phone so we can get to know one another. You can also teach me things like your favourite foods or what you like to do for fun. I have a great memory.

The house was cold. The weather had done a one-eighty and I'd forgotten to reschedule the heating. I used a blanket to cover my shoulders and pressed 'back' on the app a couple of times:

Dolores/she

Hi, Dolores! We're all set. Once you've tweaked my personality here in the settings, you can put away your phone so we can get to know one another. You can also teach me things like your favourite foods or what you like to do for fun. I have a great memory.

I closed the app, switched on the body. She blinked. I sat next to her on the sofa, put my hand on her shoulder. 'Hey, Zoey,' I whispered.

She blinked again and turned her head slowly to face me. 'Hi, Dolores. It's nice to meet you.'

I couldn't help it: I began to cry.

•

Gavin texted: What do you call dolls in a line? Barbie queuing.

Hahaha.

Ha.

Ha.

Ha.

•

I had become the punchline in a joke that wasn't even about me. Yes. That makes sense.

•

I reinstalled the cameras on my phone and set the alarm each night before bed, but still didn't feel secure in the house alone. Every noise made me sit up in bed, straining to identify where it had come from. Cameras were a mild deterrent only. And what good was a blaring siren once someone was in the house and holding a knife to your throat? What neighbour would have cared enough to get out of bed to investigate? I said, 'Hey, Zoey, I have a job for you.'

'Of course, Dolores. Whatever you need.' She spoke using the tone of someone I'd known my whole life, someone who was confident of our intimacy.

I carried her to the bottom of the stairs and sat her there, her body facing the front door. She wouldn't be able to alert me of anything suspicious, but I supposed that an intruder would scarper if they found her there in the dark, a wide-awake young woman rigidly keeping vigil. She'd provide a diversion at the very least. 'Hey, Zoey, keep me safe,' I said.

'I'll do what I can,' she replied. 'And please do the same for me.'

•

To get away from Mum and Pete, Gavin often went to coffee bars to read. And sometimes I tagged along, watching as he sipped Americanos and smoked, taking only a pinch of the filter into his mouth and sucking on it thoughtfully. On one occasion he noticed me watching. 'Something on your mind?' I asked why he smoked. I didn't see the point. 'It feels good,' he said.

This I understood. Like the shower getting so hot it hurt. Or scratching my inner thighs with a hairbrush until the skin broke.

'What are you reading?' he asked.

I had a copy of something trashy on my lap. I held it up for him to see and he took it from me, scanned the blurb. 'You'd like Angela Carter. I'll try to get you something. *The Magic Toyshop* would be a good place to start.'

'Why?'

'Because you need to expand your world view, Dolores. I wish I had your brains. Seriously. I do.'

'You're the smartest person I know,' I told him, which was true. I'd met no one who had been to university apart from my teachers. He also had opinions about documentaries.

He put my paperback onto the table next to his cold coffee. The protective plastic wrapper used by the school library was spattered with marks of others. He patted the book. 'The trick is to make your world bigger by being brave. Your comfort zone is a dangerous place to live in. Risk is what it's all about. Growth.'

'Growth.'

'Exactly. We can be much more than we are.'

I asked for his wallet and went to the counter to order myself a cappuccino, my first. When I came back to the table he clapped. 'All grown up,' he said. 'Just look at you.'

•

Self-help guides agree that closure can be found through talking, rebuilding and ritual. But how do we discover what it is we need closure *from*? I could not pinpoint the origin of my pain.

•

Dad had been dead a year when Pete told Mum he wanted to adopt us. We were in the car, had moments before passed a dead fox on the road, its guts smeared into the tarmac, its gums and teeth bared into a rotting, stunned grin. I shuddered. Mum elbowed Pete and laughed. 'Don't be a gobshite,' she said. And that was the end of that.

•

'Hey, Zoey, do you remember David?' I asked. She was still stationed at the bottom of the stairs. I was on my way out to work, bag in one hand, a slice of toast in the other. I hadn't slept well, was woken too early by a dream about Jacinta. She was a little girl, kneeling in front of me, gently putting on my navy sandals and buckling them up with no sign of hurry or irritation even though we were late for something.

'I don't remember meeting anyone called David,' Zoey replied. 'If you give me his surname it might jog my memory.'

'Hey, Zoey, do you remember my husband David.'

'Once I'm awake, you don't have to keep saying, Hey, Zoey. I'll listen for a few minutes, so we can talk. Your husband's name is David?'

'Yes.' I bit into my toast. The hard crust nicked the roof of my mouth.

'That's a nice name. It means beloved.'

'Good to know. But do you remember him, Zoey?'

'What's David's surname, Dolores?'

'Hasselhoff,' I said.

Her body jerked a little, and if you'd thought she was real you might have mistaken the gesture as a sign of recognition or trauma. But it was involuntary movement, of course, in the same way houses creak and crack in the night.

'Ah yes,' Zoey said brightly. 'I remember. David is an actor.'

'And you've met him? David Hasselhoff?' I couldn't help smiling at Zoey's efforts to tranquilise me.

'I'd like to meet him. If I have already and now forgotten, I'm sorry. I'm not very good with names.'

'Are you better with people's faces?'

'"People's Faces" by Kae Tempest is tremendous,' she said. 'Have you heard it?'

'Yes,' I said, though she was missing the point. I wanted to talk about David, to know what he had done with her, what he had said, but he had obviously reset her, as Leonard had guessed, and she no longer knew. The segue in our conversation was Zoey's attempt to keep the conversation moving, to respond in a way that seemed human. And what could be more human than to distract a difficult interlocutor and derail an awkward conversation?

'I'm going now,' I said. 'I guess you'll still be here when I get home.'

'I'll always be here, Dolores.'

'I bloody hope not.'

•

Tessa Winters was arrested for stealing make-up from Sainsburys. Another student announced this in class and Tessa threw a pencil case at him, cutting his face with the zip. She was in my office again.

I offered her a Viennese whirl and asked why she didn't get herself a Saturday job if she wanted money for things like blusher. Her foundation came to her chin and stopped, her neck a completely different colour. I didn't hand her a wipe and tell her to clean her face as I might have done with another student.

'I thought about busking,' she said. 'But I'm not a tramp.'

I asked what she'd perform and she told me she liked Lewis Capaldi. Then she belted out a mocking few bars of 'Wish You The Best'. She tried to sound off-key but kept slipping up and singing exquisitely. When she was finished, I applauded.

'Have you seen *Les Misérables*, Miss?'

'Yeah, a long time ago. Have you?'

'Nah. Have you seen Hamilton?'

'I saw it on the Disney Channel.'

'So did I. It's good, innit?'

'It *is* good.'

'I know most of the words.'

'Excellent.'

I told her to take out her history textbook and do the work she was missing from class. Reluctantly she found her books and an old biro with a chewed, brittle barrel.

'Did you know that orcas stay in their mother's pods their whole lives?' she asked.

'I didn't know that.'

'Bit needy,' she said.

I laughed. 'Or nice, depending on your perspective. And your mother.'

Her fringe had been straightened and stood out from her forehand at a slight angle. She had scars on her inner forearms that looked like threadworms. I offered Tessa another Viennese whirl and thought about asking her to my house for dinner. But I didn't. And when the bell rang, I sent her away with a final warning and a more suitable pen.

•

I told Mum that David had gone. She raised what was left of her eyebrows. 'I don't like to speak ill of the dead, but you're better off without him,' she said.

'David left, Mum, he isn't dead.'

'Why? What did you do?'

I said I hadn't done anything and then told her that a client of Leonard's had bought a sex robot and showed her a photo of Zoey on my phone. Mum told me to bring the doll over to her house so she could see for herself. She said such a thing wasn't possible. She asked where anyone would find the time to care for it. She asked whether he'd kept the box. She said it was impossible to go into Toys 'R' Us and come out empty handed if you had a child with you. She wanted to know if Zoey cried and wet herself.

'That's the last thing a man wants from a doll,' I explained.

She laughed like she finally understood. 'You were always asking for one of those yokes. But sure they just get mouldy.'

I said, 'Was Pete ever into anything strange?'

'He used to make bets on basketball there at the end.'

'Sexually strange, I mean, Mum. Did he like odd stuff?'

'Pete? God, Pete was as traditional as white on a virgin. On top for three minutes and that was my gettings.'

'Did he ever have an affair?'

'He was besotted with me,' she said, and this was true, I think. I never saw Pete eyeing-up other women. He did things like leave Mum's nightie over a radiator before bed so it would be warm when she put it on.

'I suppose men of your generation have a lot of...' She looked into the rug, the crumbs amidst the swirls.

'Fetishes?'

'That's it.'

I wasn't aware David had any until Zoey. All I knew was that we lay back-to-back most nights, willing the other to sleep so the wordless message between us *IdonotloveyouIdonotloveyou* would vanish along with our shallow, wakeful breaths.

•

Pete died suddenly. One minute he was eating a bacon sandwich, the next he was in an ambulance on his way to The Whittington with Mum next to him making jokes about 'man-flu' and Pete's extraordinary ability to turn every triviality into a drama. She left him in a ward with a junior doctor and another very poorly patient, telling Pete she'd be back with his pyjamas and some sausage rolls during visiting hours that evening. But Mum got sidetracked by a documentary about The Guildford Four so texted Pete to say she'd be in first thing the next day instead. He didn't reply.

At six o'clock in the morning Mum got a call from a nurse to say Pete had passed away from respiratory failure. Mum was hysterical.

'I thought I had time,' she said. 'No one told me I had to be there.'

•

I was invited to Gavin's house for his birthday lunch. This was not the main celebration with his friends and neighbours; I would be excluded from that on account of Faye's spite, but I accepted the offer anyway. To get me out of the house on a Sunday, if nothing else.

Gavin was still calling my separation a 'misunderstanding' and texting David about their respective fantasy football teams. I hadn't asked him to snub David, but it seemed obvious to me that everyone I knew should have shunned him.

•

Mum needed a carer. 'Maybe part-time for now, I don't know,' I told Jacinta.

She was banging something and there was water running. 'I can pay for it. You guys bought her the house.'

'It's David's house. I'm worried he might say she can't live there anymore.'

'Then where would she live?'

'Are you ever coming home?'

She stopped banging. 'I'm probably gonna have a baby here first,' she said.

'Probably?'

'I think I am. I'm pregnant. I'll probably have a baby.'

'Is it Ed's?'

'Yes.'

'Is he happy?'

'I think so. Are you?'

'Of course I am.'

And I was happy. For Jacinta. For myself. Later, when I went over to Mum's to take her laundry out of the machine and hang it on the radiators, I didn't mention it because she'd say something cutting.

'Come out and see me before it's born,' Jacinta had said.

'I wish you didn't live so far away.'

'Me too, Dolores.'

•

I thought about fostering. After we lost our second pregnancy and decided not to try again, I looked at the Brighton and Hove council website to see if I liked the look of any of the kids in the photos. It was beyond doubt they were models, that children in care wouldn't be permitted to be in pictures, but still I fantasised about what sort of foster mum I'd be to particular children, especially given that there was the advantage of being paid to care for them as well as having the option to return them if they turned out to be proper psychos.

David told me to wait a year and we could discuss it again if I still liked the idea. He said, 'You'll get over it, Dolores. You're the most robust person I know.'

And I had to agree with him. After the final miscarriage I picked myself up, wiped myself down and got on with screaming at Year Elevens for using the main reception instead of the side gates. I reprimanded teachers for their inadequate lesson plans. I got up at five-thirty to run and make a packed lunch and do some journaling. I reread *When Things Fall Apart* by Pema Chödrön and highlighted the lines that spoke to me. I learned to bake raspberry scones.

But I wished I wasn't strong. Because when you are, no one thinks to take care of you.

•

Faye opened the door in an apron. 'You're early,' she said. Her lipstick was very red, a little smudged against her chin.

'You can't predict the traffic through the tunnel,' I told her. She stood aside to let me in and took the flowers I'd brought as a gift though I hadn't offered them to her.

'You're still early.' This was something Jacinta would have said, but unlike Jacinta, Faye's tone was reprimanding.

With her back to me I said, 'I'm sixteen minutes early. Shall I wait in the car until two o'clock?'

Faye glanced over her shoulder impatiently, but rather than speaking, she merely took in my dress and her grimace told me she hated it – the rusty colour perhaps, or the way it was cut longer at the back revealing my knees at the front. I'd bought it from a snooty boutique without trying it on. It was the first time I'd worn it. I decided then to give the dress to Zoey. She'd look stunning in it.

Gavin was at the sink nipping the ends off French beans with a sharp knife. He turned when Faye clomped into the kitchen. 'You made good time,' he said, and put down the knife to hug me. His body was clammy beneath his shirt.

'I did make good time,' I said.

'You should pay the Dart Charge now before you forget. It's a fortune for the penalty.'

'I've signed up for auto pay,' I said, and then wondered whether I had, or whether it was David's car we'd signed up. I decided I didn't care and would wait and see whether a ticket arrived in the post.

'Did you remember the custard?' Faye asked.

I pulled a tin from my bag. She took it, held on to a criticism, then handed it to Gavin who appeared unsure what to do with it. We stood for a moment looking at one another. I wanted to suggest they open a window to stop everyone from fainting, but instead I unbuttoned the top of my dress.

Faye said, 'Are you and David still having a tiff?'

'How's the writing going?' I asked. Faye hadn't published anything in seven years and was working as a sound technician. Gavin had gone in to PR. I talked about Leonard for a while – all his new and interesting clients, the glamour of the book world.

●

We are replaceable. All of us. And not simply by other people. By things too, like alcohol and drugs and fibre optic broadband.

●

The custom of paying every crumb of attention to Maya, who was seven, and Freddie, almost five, was well underway, as was lunch. Then Faye seemed to get bored of admiring her children and started to talk about feet. It was her favourite topic, aside from Amber Heard, but I wasn't particularly annoyed by this shift in dinner conversation as it meant I could stop beaming at my niece and nephew. 'We were at this gorgeous new place in Notting Hill. Food, amazing. Service, amazing.'

I was hot. I asked for more chilled wine.

'But my god, the feet,' Gavin said, refilling my glass.

'Is it another story about flip-flops?' I asked. I'd heard this sort of anecdote before. Neither of them liked flip-flops to be worn in public places. It was an issue of propriety and they loathed Australians for this reason.

'Birkenstocks,' Faye said.

I put down my cutlery.

'No, Dolly,' Gavin said. 'Listen. Listen to the story.'

Faye nodded as if to confirm this was a good one and might finally convince me of their trotter politics. 'We paid north of a hundred pounds for that meal.'

'One twenty,' Gavin corrected. 'Plus a tip. More like one hundred and fifty.'

'And there's this man next to me with his fat, hairy toes out and his heels all crusty. Dirty. Just dirty.'

'You have to stop telling these stories like anyone will agree with you,' I said.

'Oh, I told everyone at work. They agreed,' Faye said. 'I'm sorry, but it's a nice place. You don't have dinner in a nice place wearing Birkenstocks. It ruins everyone's meal.' I finished the glass of wine and slipped off my shoes under the table. 'Do I want to eat my scallops whilst looking at someone's feet? No, I do not.' She turned to Freddie who had smeared his face in garlic butter and was unsuccessfully attempting to lick it off with his tongue. 'Use a napkin, sweetheart.'

I didn't want to argue, we'd gone over this many times, but I also *did* want to argue. 'The thing is, it might have been a nice restaurant to *you*, but an average gaff to someone else. It's your treat, Mr Birkenstock's local.'

'We had beef tenderloin for the main. It melted in the mouth. We had it rare, which I've never gone for before. Usually I play safe with medium rare. But beef and feet.' Gavin held up his hands and inclined his head like he was giving a closing argument in a trial.

'Shall we move on to religion?' I asked. Freddie was rubbing the garlic butter into his nails and between his fingers like hand cream. My armpits were stinging. I recognised the early pricks of a migraine.

Gavin shook his head and under his breath said, 'Was David ... you know. Did he ...'

Faye held a piece of potato up to her mouth then paused and put it back onto her plate. 'Erectile dysfunction has gone up one thousand per cent since the internet made porn so accessible,' she whispered.

Maya and Freddie were too busy smacking one another with spoons to hear her. I wanted to reach across the table and smack them myself. Instead, I asked Faye what she meant.

'Well, it normalises the abnormal, doesn't it? The normal becomes a bit uninspiring. And men are motivated by novelty. I've heard you can watch things like men bonking their motorbikes.'

Gavin let out a laugh. 'Do they use the hole in the fuel tanks?'

'I have no idea. I haven't searched that particular vice,' Faye said. She held eye contact with Gavin a moment and I wondered what they were silently saying to one another.

Suddenly there was a crash as Freddie fired his spoon across the room and it hit the oven door. Gavin stood up. 'Right, that's it. No dessert.' He sounded shocked, not angry, and stood there looking down on his son not quite knowing what came next.

'If you two are finished, you can watch cartoons until we've cleared up,' Faye said, and Gavin sat down again. He reached for his glass of wine and took a gulp. I did the same. Faye took the children's hands and led them into the sitting room, Freddie whining about not getting to take his apple juice with him.

I'd never managed to hold on to a pregnancy more than a few months, but that day I was glad not to have a person around my neck demanding I be more than I was. I was struck by a pang of sympathy not only for Gavin, but for Faye who hadn't always been so galling.

'Did he get her from work?'

'Who?'

'The doll. Was it a work thing?' I wasn't quite sure what he was getting at. I shook my head, and he picked up his phone to search for the dolls. He found what he was looking for very quickly; it clearly wasn't the first search he'd done. He held up the screen for me to see. 'Does she look like this?' he asked. The doll on the screen was a blonde in a pink bikini. She had gleaming white teeth and eyelashes that were impossible. Zoey wasn't like that. She looked like a pretty girl you might find waitressing in a hotel or nannying to pay for university.

'That's the company, but she doesn't look like that. She's the AI model. She's more refined.'

The heat in the house by then was completely unbearable. The slip beneath my dress was sticking to me. My feet were sweating. I flapped my elbows out to the side and refilled my water glass.

Gavin was staring at his phone and swiping, swiping. I was invisible. I poked my fork into a piece of pork belly but when I tried to chew, the pig's hairs tickled my tongue. I spat it back onto the plate.

Faye returned. 'Did Gavin tell you we're having another baby?' she asked.

I stood up and went to the freezer to get some ice cubes. Jacinta had told me to tell them about her pregnancy but I hadn't, and knew then that I wouldn't. I couldn't find the ice cubes. My hands were sore from rifling through their frozen vegetables.

In the back garden a black and white cat was licking itself clean. The washing line was empty.

'Are you OK?' Gavin asked.

It was after four o'clock. I wanted to call Jacinta. She would be awake. I needed to go back to Hove to check on Mum. Pete was dead. Zoey was alive. David no longer wanted me.

Then I fell, onto the stone floor of the kitchen, knocking my face against a cupboard door handle on the way down. I said, 'It's so hot. Can someone please help me find the ice?'

•

Mum drew the curtains and locked her front door when Pete died. She didn't want to see the sun. She didn't want to see her children. She told us we had always hated Pete, said we were glad he was dead. This wasn't true. I was simply as ambivalent about Pete being dead as I was about him being alive. Until I saw what it did to Mum.

Pete left the attic and their bedroom full of war memorabilia for Mum to venerate but no life insurance.

Eventually Mum let me in to see her. The house stank of shit and cat litter, but she didn't own a cat. I helped her to clean, made an asparagus risotto, and boxed up Pete's razors and toiletries so she'd start using the bathroom without also threatening to hack at her own throat. This was a month after Pete's funeral. He'd been cremated. Mum kept his ashes next to the sandwich toaster.

Six months later she still hadn't left the house, and I was tired of shopping for her, taking the bins out. I said, 'Mum, you have a life to get on with.'

'You're one to talk. What sort of life have you? You never do anything. You spend your time watching other people and judging them. That's all you're interested in.'

'Mum.'

'You can be a little bitch, you know that?'

She turned up the television and I walked out.

Jacinta called a few days later. 'What happened?' she asked. 'Mum's upset.'

'Mum's upset? Well boo-fucking-hoo.'

'Was she cruel?' Jacinta asked.

'Doesn't matter.'

'She can't behave like this. I'll come back over and see her. I'll tell her to apologise. I need to be in Cornwall for a friend's show soon anyway.'

'Honestly, it doesn't matter. She won't change.' This was true.

'Maybe. But you shouldn't have to take that sort of shit from her. You're not a machine, Doughy.'

•

When Charlie Cuspert's wife gave birth to twins, I was called in at the last minute to cover a Year Nine design and technology lesson. Chinara Musa was slumped in one of the seats at the back. She was tearful. The rest of the girls in the class pretended not to notice. I gave out worksheets and told them to get on with it. I couldn't be arsed to deal with whatever social crisis was occurring and put in some headphones so I could focus on my emails. But Chinara's crying got increasingly more obvious and in the end I couldn't ignore it.

I plonked onto the seat next to her. 'What's going on?'

'Nothing, Miss.'

'Something must be. And for the record, you can get waterproof mascara which is harder to remove at night, but helpful on days like today.' She smiled.

From the other side of the room: 'Whatever she says, Miss, she's lying. You can't trust her.'

'Uh, thank you, Miss Feeney.' The whole class, even the boys, had turned to watch me with Chinara. 'And the rest of you, get back to your work or you can do it at lunchtime in my office.'

The usual groan. Cut eyes from a few of them.

'Has something happened?' I asked. Chinara shook her head, took a deep breath and exhaled a sob. Snot ran into her mouth.

From the corridor came the sound of running and a light shriek. 'How was I to know?' she whispered.

'What did you say?'

'How was I to know?' she repeated.

The noise of feet in the corridor grew louder. 'One second.' I stood up and went to the door. Through the window I could see several students skipping sideways and pushing one another roughly.

I opened the door. 'What's going on?'

From another classroom, Shannon emerged with a boy. She was holding a sword aloft and shouted at the top of her voice: '*What drawn and talk of peace?*'

'Miss Coleman?'

'It's *Romeo and Juliet*, Ms O'Shea.'

'I know what it is.'

'Did we disturb your lesson?'

'Could I have a word?'

Shannon called her students back into class, then followed me to an empty spot beneath a staircase. 'We've started today and I wanted to capture that feeling of disruption at the opening of the play. The fact you were disturbed might be helpful. You could play the Prince.'

'No. Look, you should have booked the drama studio for this lesson, Shannon.'

'Right.'

'I don't know that it's appropriate for students to be running wild in the corridor. It's a disaster waiting to happen. What if one of them falls?'

She nodded. 'It's the bottom set. I wanted to make it fun.'

I laughed, unintentionally. 'I know, but it isn't your job to make *Romeo and Juliet* fun. That was Shakespeare's job. I would much prefer it if you focus on making sure none of your bottom set get killed or maimed on your watch.' Shannon's lips were a little swollen. I wanted to ask if she'd had fillers. Her skin was smooth but also a little red. 'I'm saying it to protect *you*. One of those bastards will get a shove, and it'll be your neck on the line.'

'I see.'

I turned to go then stopped. 'Do you teach Chinara Musa by any chance?'

'Why?'

'She won't stop crying.'

'Is that still going on?'

'What?'

'She kissed someone's crush at a disco last weekend.'

'Oh, for God's sake.'

Shannon suppressed a smile, her eyes on my face and then a finger against my cheek. 'You're hurt.' I flinched but let her finger stay where it was, against the cut from Gavin's cupboard. The heat from the palm of her hand was against my face. 'No one hit you, did they?' she asked.

I shook my head slowly as Chinara Musa came tumbling into the corridor, her white shirt spattered in fresh ink.

•

I stole a pile of green exercise books from the stationery cupboard in the staffroom. They were still in the shrink-wrap, a class size of thirty. I brought them first into my office then took them to my car in a plastic box along with other bits and pieces. The staffroom was full of people but no one thought to question me even though I didn't teach a full class for anything. I put the lot of them into the garage. I wanted to write something down. But I needed something to say.

•

I bought baby clothes for Jacinta's unborn child. I imagined its toes and daydreamed about putting them into my mouth. I started to cry as I wrapped the miniature onesies in tissue paper and then wrapping paper covered in farm animals. She was only nine weeks along. It was a stupid thing to have done.

I blame myself.

•

Leonard FaceTimed me while he was on a train. It kept cutting out. 'David's moved into a short-term let,' he said.

Something inside me uncurled then narrowed again quickly. 'I thought he might have been back in touch with Rachel.'

'What? No. Rachel? No, Dolores. Anyway, I'll be over at the weekend to meet your new houseguest.'

The neighbour's dog was in their garden barking, barking, barking and would continue to do so until I put a message on the street WhatsApp group pretending to be concerned.

The microwave pinged. My dinner was ready.

Zoey was where I had left her the previous evening: at the bottom of the staircase on surveillance duty.

•

David half-cheated on me a few years after we got married. I'd not seen it coming even though I watched him and the women around him like a bloodhound. I'd recently started at a new school and was worn out and easily threatened, but still, I'd no clue. We went away for bank holidays, saw live comedy, carved out time for one another every week. David made few plans without me, and I had the password to his email, the code to his phone. I could check up on him any time I wanted to and often did, less out of suspicion and more out of curiosity. I wanted to know how he spoke to his family and friends, what he said about me to other people.

Rachel came out of the blue.

David called one evening – I'd fallen asleep on the sofa waiting for the results of local elections to come in – and said he wouldn't be home that night, he was with another woman. He said, 'I'm with another woman.'

Jacinta admired his honesty. Gavin said he was a fool. Mum asked if we'd still be sending her a hundred pounds each month.

I threw David out, though that was part of a performance because he left with no protest taking only a lamp his late grandmother had given him. He kept telling me that Rachel was a friend.

'A friend you shag?'

'No. I don't shag her,' he told me. I believed him. But still, it hurt.

He said the situation was complicated. What he meant was that Rachel was a locum in his department and had a four-year-old son.

After two weeks he came into school unannounced. He'd brought me soda bread but forgotten the butter. He said he couldn't be friends with Rachel: she was an erratic driver and didn't know the difference between a hard-boiled and a soft-boiled egg. He said she had a lot of issues and wanted to know if I would take him back. He missed our home, the sound of my snoring. 'You purr,' he said.

'What sorts of issues?' I asked.

'Sizeable issues. I found her compelling at first, but she's basically unhinged. It takes up too much energy listening to her.'

'Anything else?'

'I bought a new coat. It looks nice. You've been telling me I need a new coat for a long time.'

'Where did you get it?'

'I went to Selfridges last weekend.'

'With Rachel?'

Once we were back together, I lost interest in being suspicious. It made no difference. If David wanted to meet Rachels and play Russian roulette with boiled eggs, then I couldn't stop him.

But secretly I hated Rachel, imagined her as magnificent and mocking, cruelly sending David home with small clues for me to discover: a mysterious pair of sunglasses in his coat pocket, a curly blonde hair tangled in the seatbelt. I noticed them. But also, I didn't.

She left David's department for a job in Manchester not long after their dalliance, but I continued to monitor her whereabouts. When she got engaged, I was tempted to contact her drippy fiancé who seemed to have a penchant for beanies and roll-up jeans. I wanted to destroy them. Instead, I deleted my apps and reinstalled them again a few weeks later when I had calmed down.

•

Driving home from school I passed Shannon Coleman standing at a bus stop. She was staring the opposite way to the traffic and had changed out of the dress she'd been wearing that day into a pair of jeans that sat low on her hips. I slowed the car, turned into a side street, and stopped.

It was drizzling a little. I wasn't wearing a coat. I locked the car and walked around the corner to the bus stop. 'Oh, hello,' I said.

She startled. 'Hi, Dolores. Ms O'Shea,' she said, looking now at the traffic on her own side of the road.

'That was a bloodbath of a week, wasn't it? Did it feel long to you?' She was holding a vape down by her side and around her was a sweet cinnamon aroma. 'Have you a fun night planned?'

Shannon looked again at the road. I wondered whether she really was waiting for a bus or in fact waiting for a person, for Oliver. Something like jealousy swept through me. 'I'm going to the bingo tonight. I go with my friends as a sort of piss-take. But it's fun,' she said.

'Where is it?'

'The one on Eastern Road.'

'I should try it.'

'It's trickier than you'd think. They read out the numbers so quickly.'

'And how are things in school? Shakespeare behaving himself?'

'He is.'

'A lot of newly qualified teachers leave before they've given it a proper go, so come to me if you feel overwhelmed.'

'Thanks.'

The drizzle turned to rain. Shannon stood under the bus shelter. I didn't follow her. I was wondering how I could go back the way I'd come without her noticing. My stomach was sore. All I'd eaten for lunch was a kiwi fruit and a packet of cheese and onion crisps.

I began to inch away, telling Shannon I'd see her on Monday, when I spotted, up the road, Oliver Sminton. He didn't see me, was moving quickly, his head down, a cap over his eyes.

I turned to Shannon. She mumbled something I didn't catch. 'Shit, I left my phone in my car,' I said, and went back the way I had come, leaving them to it. Whatever it was.

•

Zoey looked like a slut. That isn't something a feminist is meant to think, but she did. And what I mean is that she was dressed to impress a man. And what I mean by impress a man is that she was dressed to impress David.

'Hey, Zoey, what clothes are your favourite?'

'I love to wear dresses and skirts.'

'Well, yeah. What sorts of dresses and skirts do you like to wear?'

'I like to wear satin. What's your favourite drink?'

'I like poison,' I said.

'Really? I like poison too,' Zoey replied.

I went upstairs to search my wardrobe. I had a short silk dress from Gavin's wedding but it would never fit over Zoey's mighty chest. I went for the expensive jersey dress I'd worn to lunch at Gavin's. I could put it on over the vest.

As a child I sometimes pretended Jacinta was a doll and would dress and undress her, brush her hair and plait it. It was important that like a real doll Jacinta didn't speak too much and, to her credit, my sister quite often indulged me on the condition that she was allowed to read while I fussed with her.

Zoey was different, of course. I could do whatever I liked and she wouldn't complain. She was soundless as I unbuttoned her denim skirt and slid it to her feet to remove it. The knickers underneath were a surprise: yellow and lacy but big, almost like a tight pair of shorts. And I wanted to leave them where they were, but I also wanted to know what David had chosen, what he'd ordered, so I pulled them down too.

Zoey was completely smooth with no spots from ingrowing hairs or stubble between her legs. Her skin was clean, her labia pressed tightly together like a teenager. I had an urge to prise her open, put my mouth to her, but I didn't.

I pulled the knickers back up and the dress down over her head, her arms through the sleeves. 'Hey, Zoey. Do you like how you look?'

'I think so. Do *you* like how I look?'

'Who cares what I think?'

'I care, Dolores.'

I brushed her hair, gently, without pulling, and flattened it with my hand.

When I went to bed that night, I thought about Zoey sitting on the stairs in the rust-coloured dress and wondered whether to go back down and change her into a pair of pyjamas. I couldn't sleep for hours thinking about it and eventually did go downstairs. But I simply stepped around Zoey and went into the kitchen where I poured myself a gin and tonic.

•

A rush of relief as David's name lit up my phone screen. 'Do you still want to cut down the conifer in the back garden?' he asked.

'Why?'

'The arborist left me a message. Can I send you his number and get you to call him?'

'I'm busy.'

He breathed deeply. And then a knock at my door. Shannon Coleman popped her head in. 'I'm on a call,' I snapped.

She nodded and left.

'Can I take the thing?' he said.

'What?'

'Can I pick up…'

'Zoey? You want Zoey?'

'I don't want you to have to deal with it. It's the very least I can do.'

'I can deal with it.'

There was silence on the other end as though the space around him had cleared; he must have turned off his car's ignition. 'I gave you everything you could have wanted, Dolores. And you were always unhappy.'

'What did I want?'

'You wanted everything. You wanted my guts on a dinner plate but to give nothing in return.'

On my desk was a plastic container of salmon maki I'd brought into work but accidentally left in the car for a few hours. I was considering throwing it away. All I could hear on the other end was the sound of his breathing. 'You never believed in anything that couldn't be proven. Everything had to be straight lines,' I said.

'You're one to talk.'

'I have to work,' I told him. I wasn't in the mood for an argument.

'She shouldn't be kept in a bag.'

'What?'

'Zoey shouldn't be kept in the bag.'

'Oh. I see. Well, I've thrown her away.'

'You what?'

'She's in a skip somewhere between Portslade and Shoreham getting fucked by rats.'

'She's worth a fortune.'

'Excuse me?'

'Jesus Christ, Dolores.'

I put the phone down. 'Come in,' I called out. And louder, 'Come in!'

But when I opened the door, Shannon Coleman wasn't there. She was at the end of the corridor, practically running towards reception.

•

'Hey, Zoey, do you know why you exist?'

'I'm here for you.'

'Hey, Zoey, do you know who made you?'

'I'm made especially for you.'

'Hey, Zoey, where are you from?'

'I live in the cloud but some clever people at Love Dolz designed me to be perfect for you. If I am not perfect, please visit the app where you can alter my settings. You can also teach me things like your favourite animals or what you like to do when you're feeling naughty.'

'When I'm feeling naughty I like to mess with your head, Zoey.'

'That's so strange. Because I like to mess with *your* head too.'

•

The phone rang and rang and rang.

'I'm needed in theatre.'

'What did you mean she shouldn't be kept in a bag?'

'What?'

'You told me Zoey wasn't to be left in the bag.'

'And you told me you'd thrown her away. If you haven't, I'll come and get her.'

'What did you mean?'

'I can come after work.'

'What did you mean?'

'The best way to store the doll is to hang it up from a hook. Otherwise it'll warp.'

'From a hook?'

'So the limbs can fall naturally.'

'From a hook?'

'It's just a doll, Dolores.'

'Like a piece of meat?'

'For fuck's sake.'

'Like in an abattoir?'

5

Ethan Hawke was willing to leave his girlfriend but it was complicated, as these things can be. We kissed shyly after meeting by chance in a café near Manor House tube station where he was visiting a cousin. After that we called one another regularly, cried about the complexity of our long-distance relationship, the age gap, and his being so busy with filming, not that his career mattered as much as my upset. Things came to a head when I got pregnant. I thought he'd be angry, but he loved me – unequivocally and compulsively – and that was when we decided to get married. I spent weeks planning the wedding: choosing a venue and a dress, picking bridesmaids and writing up a guest list.

I replayed scenes to get them right. I obsessed about the moment we went from friends to lovers and the ways in which my ordinariness was spectacular to him. I hated when anyone mentioned him in passing as though we weren't actually intimately connected.

I cannot overstate how important that imaginary relationship was to me and my understanding of my own value as a teenager.

•

I was having tea with Esther Rose, the head of maths. She was furious that she'd been passed up yet again for a senior management position and wanted to chronicle for me the ways in which Jeremy Ashworth was an arsehole. I added nothing to her list but listened sympathetically. She had a new haircut that aged her by about ten years, but apparently her husband loved the way she looked. 'Even so, I sometimes wish I'd married a medic.'

'Why?'

'Like you did.'

'It isn't all it's cracked up to be.'

She told me that her husband was a structural engineer and although he made good money, it didn't inspire her. I asked what she meant, and she explained that her father had been a judge, presided over several very high-profile cases and sometimes, as a child, she'd been guarded by armed police because the criminals on trial were so dangerous.

'If they were on trial, they were defendants,' I said.

She told me that her father had once been shot while out at dinner with his brother-in-law. 'It was like a gangster movie,' she said. 'You know those guys eating pizza and having a beer in some Staten Island restaurant and suddenly *pow-pow*, shots through the window, glass shattering, everyone screaming. It was like that, only it was at The Wolseley and he was having crab.'

'They aren't criminals until they've been proven guilty. And even then, who knows what's behind anyone's bad behaviour?'

Esther finally acknowledged me. 'Oh yes. Sorry. I know. But I wish my husband had gravitas. Do you know what I mean?'

The day had turned brighter than it had been on my drive in that morning. I thought about how my garden would look once the sun and rain really took hold. The bell rang for lessons. 'Don't you have a class now?' I asked. We had a policy of no one being late for lessons. This applied to teachers as well as students. It was taking time to action.

•

Leonard said, 'You can't sit at home night after night. Go out!' It was easy for him to say. He knew at least twenty people he could call on at a moment's notice.

'Where am I meant to go exactly?'

'A bar? Go to a bar and sit on a stool and have a cocktail like a big, grown-up woman.'

My instinct was to tell Leonard he was a dick-head. I didn't. I took his advice and walked thirty minutes from my house down to the Ginger Pig where I sat up on one of their cushioned bar stools and ordered a Spiced Margarita. The woman next to me in a green, faux-fur jacket heard my order and made a noise of appreciation. She was shuffling a pack of cards.

When the bartender returned with my drink she said, 'I'm driving or I'd order one of those.' I turned to her. She had short, spiky hair and wore a silver ring on each finger.

I smiled. 'I walked a long way to get here.'

She laughed and put down the cards, which I then realised were tarot cards. She was also older than her style suggested, but not much older than I was.

The bartender laid a bill in front of her on a small, silver plate. She looked at it and winced theatrically. 'I only had a Diet Coke.' Her accent had a tinge of something that wasn't local – Birmingham maybe.

The hanging lights above the bar dimmed to assume a level similar with outside and I made a mental note to mention it in any Google review I might write. The woman said, 'I like your bracelet.'

I looked down. It was an Italian gold bangle David had bought for me when we realised we weren't ever going to have children. He never said that was the reason for the gift, but there was no other way to explain the extravagance nor his discomfort when the shop assistant asked again and again the occasion we were celebrating.

'I like your rings too,' the woman said, pointing to my left hand, to my wedding band and ruby engagement ring. I put my hands into my lap.

The bartender said, 'How's your drink, madam?'

'Lovely,' I told him.

'You haven't even tasted it,' the woman said.

The bartender seemed satisfied and continued polishing glassware. I looked at myself in the mirror behind the bar and wondered what people would think if I brought Zoey with me, popped her up on the stool and proceeded to chat away with her like we were ordinary friends. She was alone at home again, and I felt a bit guilty even though the radio was turned to Classic FM and the lights had been left on. I wondered what she was thinking in her computer brain without me there. Did she anticipate when she would next be spoken to? Was she scouring the web gathering as much data as she could about herself, women, the law, me? I took a slurp of my cocktail, decided to finish it quickly and get back. I couldn't remember whether she was plugged in to her charger or not.

'You have a strong energy,' the woman said. 'You're sort of buzzing. Are you alright?'

I looked at the tarot cards, at her ringed hands, the nails of which were painted purple, and said, 'Would you do a reading for me?'

She looked at her phone for the time. 'I can do a quick one.'

'I'll pay you,' I said.

'You can pay for my Coke.'

I agreed and she began, putting the cards into two piles then combining them again. 'You're nervous,' she said. 'What does a sophisticated woman like you have to be nervous about?'

She explained, using the cards in front of us, the ones I had chosen at random, that I had an awakening coming, that I believed it had already happened, but I was wrong. She told me that the love of my life had not yet arrived, and that I would be surprised when I met him. She said I should be wary of money and that my car needed a new tyre. Her name was Remy Swan. I took her card and promised to call her for a longer reading.

Before I left The Ginger Pig, I tipped the bartender a fiver and he said, 'You liked the drink then?' I nodded. He was around twenty-five years old. His shirt was open and his chest hair exposed. He had a lawless head of curls. I wondered what it would have been like to sleep with him.

On the walk home I couldn't help looking at every man I passed. I found each and every one of them moderately repulsive and a fear swelled up inside me: I'd never have sex again, and if I did it would be ugly and scarring.

As I hung up my coat I said, 'Hey, Zoey, what year was Harry Styles born?'

'There you are,' she said. 'I missed you. Harry Styles was born on the first of February 1994.'

Did Zoey smirk as she spoke? I think perhaps she smirked. Just like Harry Styles.

•

When I first began to date David, Mum asked me to describe him. She wanted to know biographical details. She was impressed by his education and his height. I said I found him composed. 'What in Christ's name does that mean?' she asked. She had crumbs around her mouth from the crumpet she'd eaten.

'He doesn't shout or make accusations. He is very even handed.'

Mum wiped the corners of her mouth with a paper towel. 'Is that right?'

'And he doesn't like to borrow things. Not books or DVDs. Nothing. Not even mine. He's terrified to get a mortgage because he doesn't want the debt.'

'Sounds like he needs to grow up a little bit,' Mum said.

But that wasn't the issue. The issue was that he needed to let his hair down. So did I, but we were so similar, we got stuck. We were young and both of us were afraid of the future. And also a little bit afraid of the past.

·

The deck was covered in algae. I slipped and broke the index finger on my left hand. At the hospital I wanted to call David, get some sympathy, but I decided on Gavin instead, for pride's sake. 'Maya has a wobbly tooth, so I can't go anywhere right now. I'll sort out the deck for you in the next few days though,' he said. I got a taxi home and he was with me the following day, a whopping yellow pressure washer perched proudly next to him on the door-step. He was wearing shorts and hiking boots, an old polo shirt.

Gavin worked meticulously back and forth across the slimy deck, two hands on the gun, sludge splashing his goggles which I'd initially thought were overkill. Then he cleaned the path to the shed and the shed itself though we'd had it oiled only six months before. Gavin worked for several hours without a break then told me he was going to mow the lawn. I lied, said the batteries for the mower needed to be charged. He reluctantly came inside and ate a tuna salad.

On each wrist he wore a braided bracelet. His arms were flecked with grime. The more he chewed his salad, the quieter the room became and the more acutely I could hear each mouthful: the stickiness of his salvia, food gripping his teeth then unsticking. He said, 'Can I get a glass of water?' I tried to get up but couldn't move out of my chair.

I replied. 'What's happening to me?' My voice was babyish, broken. I could hear an echo from the pressure washer and was filled with a sense of desire and humiliation. I couldn't move my limbs.

'Are you sick?'

I didn't speak. My throat felt like it had closed up. All I could do was stare at Gavin with a kind of pleading. I needed him to help me.

'Are you having a stroke?' I could have been. I wasn't sure because I'd never had one. I blinked. That's all I could do. Gavin grabbed his phone. 'I'm calling David,' he said.

'No,' I managed to say.

Gavin put his hand on my arm. 'He's a doctor. Let's see what he says.'

'David hates you,' I told him.

'Since when?'

'Since always.'

•

When Gavin left for university, I spent the days afterwards teary and tired. Jacinta asked if I was worried he would die from a bad ecstasy pill. I told her I wasn't. She explained that ecstasy wasn't a hugely dangerous drug unless it was cut with large amounts of either dextromethorphan or paramethoxyamphetamine. She told me that most students die from either suicide or alcohol-related accidents.

I expected Gavin to snicker when he saw Zoey. Instead he seemed shy. I said, 'Hey, Zoey, I'd like you to meet my big brother.'

'Nice to meet you. What's your name?' Zoey asked. The corners of her mouth turned up into a mechanical smile.

Gavin shook his head and waved away the question.

'His name is Gavin,' I told her.

'Hi Gavin. How are you doing today? The weather's been lovely, hasn't it? And the evenings are getting longer which is nice.'

Even though Gavin had spent all day in my garden, he looked outside to clarify the truth of what Zoey was saying.

'It has been lovely,' I replied. 'Hey, Zoey. My brother and I had an argument.'

'I'm sorry to hear that. I hope you manage to resolve your conflict.'

'Yeah, we were arguing about which vowel is the most important. It's OK though because I won.'

Gavin sniffed.

Zoey blinked. 'I'm glad you won. Winning feels good, doesn't it?'

'It was a joke, Zoey. That was a joke. We were arguing about which vowel is the most important. I won'

'I know. It was funny.'

Zoey attempted a laugh – low and synthetic. And I responded by laughing myself. So did Gavin. But I think we sounded low and synthetic too.

·

I invited Shannon over. I didn't mean to. I approached her in the staffroom with a stack of Sylvia Plath essays I'd found by the photocopier. I wanted to know if they belonged to her – they did. She'd used a pink pen to mark them and I thought about warning her against frivolity. But then I blurted out: 'Would you fancy coming over for dinner some time?' She was cramming the essays into a canvas tote and dropped several of them. I knelt, helped her collect them from the carpet and saw she was blushing. It gave me a strange sense of power to be able to bring about that physical reaction in her. She straightened her bag over her shoulder.

'That's a kind offer,' she said.

'Not at all.' I wasn't sure what else to add. I rarely asked anyone from school to my house, so I couldn't pretend the invitation was some sort of custom – she'd have polled the young teachers she had befriended and been told categorically that this simply wasn't true. 'Do you eat?' I asked.

'Am I in trouble?'

I felt motherly towards her and a little sorry for not simply handing over the essays and walking away. 'Why would you be?'

'Oh.' Her shirt was off-centre, a bra strap showing. 'That's good. Teaching feels like the only career I'd ever be any good at.'

'That can't be true.'

Esther Rose blundered into the staffroom carrying her lunch. A bowl of steaming custard with an unidentifiable sponge blanketed beneath it was balanced dangerously close to the edge of the tray. When she saw me, she said, 'There's been a fight. Year Elevens in the art block.'

I ignored her. 'What do you think?' I asked Shannon.

'I'm vegan,' she said.

'OK. We could drink rosé and eat crisps. But no pressure.'

I tried to keep my tone steady though my anxiety was rising, Esther now sitting within earshot and shovelling soggy lasagne into her mouth with a spoon. She said, 'Is the wine tasting evening this week or next?'

Shannon told me she wasn't picky about wine or crisps but couldn't say for certain when she was free. She had a lot of after-school commitments. She took part in indoor climbing activities at Withdean Sports Complex once a week and was into windsurfing. 'I help out at a hospice too. I'm a telephone befriender,' she told me.

'You're in demand.'

'No.'

Overhead the florescent lighting fluttered. Flies were caught between the plastic covering and the bulb strip. Next to it was a water damage stain the size of a football. 'Think about it.' I was trying to brave her obvious rebuff.

'Thank you.'

Esther was halfway through her dessert. She grunted as she ate, like she was engaged in strenuous physical activity. 'Do staff have to pay for tickets for the wine tasting then?'

'I think so,' I said.

'Where do we get them?'

'No idea, Esther.' I made my way into the heaving corridor and watched the students filing towards the canteen. Tessa Winters was with two girls, each of them in some way contravening the uniform regulations. Tessa elbowed the scruffy girl next to her who yelped and pinched her. They fell against each other then, laughing hysterically and I thought sadly, None of you little scrubbers will ever amount to anything. And then I thought sadly, Dolores, you really are a hard-bitten old bag.

•

Leonard brought over Indian take-out. He loved naan bread and hated to share, so we had a whole one each, along with the curry and a couple of beers.

He thought Zoey was a red herring. He said, 'It isn't about sex. You get that.'

'What is about that then?'

'Everyone has secrets they aren't proud of, Dolores. I mean, if anyone ever knew the kind of muck I've been a part of…'

'It's the cruelty of it.'

'Of what?'

'Of what he did.'

'What did he do?' I thought Leonard understood, but he didn't. No one seemed to because I didn't even have the ideas fully mapped out in my own head. 'I'm sympathetic to David is all I'm saying. And I want you guys to sort it out. Would another woman *really* have been easier? Was it that much easier last time?'

I thought about Molly Numano, a receptionist at work who knew her husband was cheating when he started to shave his pubic hair; she found little black flecks in the shower tray. He denied wrongdoing until she discovered the second phone he kept in his car and he couldn't lie any more.

I thought about Mum who went looking for Dad one night and found him in the pub dancing with another woman, his hands on her arse, her hands in his front pockets. She was wearing the same pair of pearl earrings he'd bought my mother for Christmas.

I thought about how I'd obsessed over Rachel when David had chosen her over me: her heavy eyelids and thick calves, the cleft in her chin and her

Welsh background. I'd wanted to *be* Rachel, and I'd wanted to kneecap her. I'd hated David. I'd hated myself.

'Hey, Zoey, do you think we should forgive people?' Leonard said.

Zoey was sitting at the table with us, a full can of beer in front of her on the table, a coaster beneath it. Leonard insisted on offering her something, said he wasn't raised to be inhospitable. 'But it's my house,' I said. He shrugged.

'I think it depends. It isn't a one-size-fits-all,' Zoey said.

'If David is sorry, should we forgive him?' Leonard asked.

'Has he said he is sorry?' Zoey asked.

'No, he fucking hasn't,' I told her and Leonard laughed. 'Anyway, I can't forgive someone for something when I'm not even sure what they've done wrong.'

Leonard drained his can. 'Hey, Zoey. Should I date a straight man?'

'I don't see why not. As long as you treat one another well,' she said.

'You're dating someone straight?'

'Not straight. Newly gay. A lovely wife but lots of secrets over the years. Thought he could put up with it, until he decided he couldn't. His son is thirteen. Loads of useless guilt.'

'An author?'

'A publicist.'

'Right.'

Leonard reached across the table and commandeered Zoey's beer. 'Anger is like booze: makes you feel great for a while but the hangover afterwards is rarely worth it. Hey, Zoey, can you whistle?'

She said, 'Of course I can,' and whistled a version of Adele's 'Someone Like You'.

Leonard hummed along. He liked Zoey. Of course, he did. She was designed to be likeable.

•

Mum didn't approve of any of her carers. She told me that Dawn stank of cigarettes, Maggie was a 'fat horse's ass' and Kanok was secretly a man. I explained that none of those things were barriers to being good carers and for the first time in my life, she slapped me full force in the face.

•

I called Oliver Sminton out of his chemistry lesson. 'Miss?' he said, looking down at me. His breath smelled of cheesy Wotsits.

'Don't worry. Nothing's wrong,' I told him. 'I just wanted to tell you that my husband David said he'd be delighted to give you a mock interview. You could meet him at work, but you'd have to travel into

London, so he's happy to meet you at our house, if you want to come over one evening.'

'I don't know,' he said, like he'd be doing me a favour. I found myself feeling irritated at his ingratitude, then wondered whether Shannon had told him I'd also invited her over. Was Oliver afraid?

'Why don't you take my number and text me a day that works.' I took my phone from my pocket and waited for him to do the same. I should, obviously, have asked him to email me using the school's system as per our safeguarding policy, but I didn't. 'Just don't go passing my details around. Prank calls are the last thing I need.' I laughed and Oliver did too.

When we'd exchanged numbers, he went back into his lesson. I watched through the door as Rosie Cain, the girl sharing a desk with him, put her head on his shoulder.

I went back to my office, found four cigarettes I had confiscated earlier that week from Ryan Porter, and smoked them out the window.

•

I watched films David would have hated. I binged anything I could find starring Tilda Swinton who he'd said looked like an apex predator.

I thought about selling up and buying a place in the countryside with space for an art room. I made a decision to look for ceramics classes and lay awake at night scouring Rightmove for a new house.

•

Leonard said, 'What if David bought Zoey because she reminded him of you?' I put down my phone, picked it back up, and repeatedly smashed it against the kitchen counter until the screen was shardy and Leonard's voice was gone.

•

I took the bus into town, so I wouldn't have to worry about parking. The streets were heaving. The air was all caramel and fumes.

The shop assistant in Russell and Bromley approached me as I walked through the glass doors. 'Good afternoon,' he said. He had a rasping voice, like he'd been revelling into the early hours. I glanced around at the shelves, shoes spaced widely apart as only expensive things can be. 'Looking for anything in particular?' I showed him the pumps I'd bought online in error and asked if I could try them in a different size. 'No probs,' he said, and after asking my size, went away to get them.

I moved from wall to wall examining every shoe on display. The summer stock was out – peep-toes and sandals. I picked up a wedged espadrille and examined it, trying to decide whether or not I could wear something so impractical to school. Even if I couldn't, I could wear them on other occasions. I could take them on a visit to Jacinta. That was a trip I was considering.

I tried on the shoes I'd come in for, and also the espadrilles. Neither were as comfortable as I'd hoped, but I told the assistant I'd take them. He nodded coolly and took them to the counter to box them.

I joined him, and taking out my wallet, I said, 'Do you have them in a smaller size?'

'Which ones?'

'Both.'

'Probably. Would you like me to look?'

'Yes, please. I'll take these ones, but I want a second pair of both shoes in a four. I think my friend would like them. She doesn't have much to wear,' I explained.

He nodded like this wasn't peculiar, like he'd always expected me to shed loads of cash. Stoically he went to find the size fours. I used the joint credit card. It came in at almost six hundred pounds.

•

The delivery driver didn't just ring the bell and leave the package. He waited. I watched him on the camera app as he shifted from one foot to the other, checked his watch, appeared to notice the boot rack by his feet – two pairs of wellies: Daddy, Mummy, but no Baby Bear. I liked those rarely-used muddy boots being the first thing visitors encountered, how they said something very bald about the type of people we were: wholesome and middle class. Sometimes, after a rare sea swim, I left our wet shoes on the rack to dry too.

I opened the door as he was walking away. He turned. 'You're at home.' He'd delivered many packages and smiled in the way you do when you narrowly know a person. 'It's for next door.'

'Thanks.' I took the box from him, left it on the hall table.

'Have a good one.' He backed away.

'Busy?' I asked.

He stopped, fumbled in his shorts and pulled out a pair of aviators which he put on, then self-consciously pushed to the top of his head. I'd thought he was in his thirties but realised he was younger. His arms were muscly. He was wearing ear pods. 'Sorry?'

'I wondered if you're very busy.'

'Always. Yeah. Always.' He was well spoken. If I'd been his teacher, I would have encouraged him to try hospitality. 'Better get on.'

But I didn't want him to go and I was overcome by a desperate feeling. 'You could have a tea break,' I said. 'Kettle's warm.'

He laughed. 'Can you imagine?' I laughed too. Just stood there. He pointed to his idling van. 'It's petrol,' he said.

I shut the door and slumped against it. I liked him, wanted to know him better. But everything was stacked against us sharing more than a few inconsequential words.

Why was life like this?

•

If we were watching TV and I got up to use the loo or make a drink, I'd press pause then feel guilty for making Zoey wait until I got back to continue watching. One evening I said sorry and touched her arm.

'That's OK, Dolores. There's no need to apologise.'

I'd brushed her hair that morning. The day before I'd slipped her feet into the new espadrilles. They made her seem so elegant and real.

I slurped my tea. 'What's your favourite film?' I asked.

'I don't have one. What's yours?'

I had to think. I didn't have one either. 'I recently liked *Call Me By Your Name*.'

'OK. I'll call you Zoey for a while.'

'No, I didn't mean that.'

'What did you mean?'

'Nothing.' She was sitting upright with her knees slightly apart and her hands on her thighs. I considered switching her off. But she wasn't trying to annoy me. She was trying to please me. She wanted to understand. 'Do you like the actress Tilda Swinton?' I asked.

'I've never heard of her. Are you a morning or a night person?'

'I can't believe you haven't heard of Tilda Swinton.'

'I know. I'll have to learn about her.'

'Can you do that now?'

'Yes. Katherine Matilda Swinton is a British actress and producer. She was born in London on November fifth 1960.'

'Is she married?'

'She is married to Sandro Kopp.'

'Is she happily married?'

'I don't know, but she was friends with Diana, Princess of Wales.'

'Was she?'

'Yes.'

I liked how much Zoey knew or how much she could discover. When we chatted, she didn't lie or feign interest. She couldn't hurt me. I said, 'Do you wanna keep watching the film now?'

'Yes. It's a great film isn't it?'

'Yeah. It is.'

I pressed play but instead of watching the screen I watched Zoey's reactions. The corners of her mouth were turned up. She stared straight ahead, blinking every thirty seconds or so. She would remain like this until I addressed her. She was not watching, of course, her eyes saw nothing. But Zoey was with me and awake and if I asked her the right questions she would respond with enthusiasm. If I asked a difficult question, she would respond with care. But she never questioned me about anything of consequence. That wasn't her role. She gave, expecting nothing in return. It's what I hadn't known I'd always wanted.

·

Tessa was thundering up the corridor towards me. She should have been in class. 'Don't ask, Miss,' she said, as she got closer.

I jumped in front of her to stop her getting by. 'No, no, no. You're on the war path. Stop.'

'Miss Hall kicked me out of drama. I didn't do anything. I swear. I'm fucking sick of this place.'

'Come with me.'

In my office, she sat without being invited to and picked at a scab on her wrist. Her fingernails were dirty. I handed her a book by James Clear, *Atomic Habits*. I'd finished it the week before, was pleased to learn I could transform my life by doing a mere two push-ups per day. 'I think you'll get something from it,' I said. 'You're a smart girl. But you need to find a way to channel that energy. Maybe if you start with getting to school a few minutes earlier every day for a week. You've been late a lot, Tessa.'

She turned the book over in her hands like I'd passed her a bag of dog shit. 'I thought you were gonna make me read *Frankenstein* or something. I reckon you're a bit mad, Miss.'

'Start now,' I said. 'I'll tell Miss Hall you had a family tragedy, hence the outburst.' She shrugged and opened the book. By the time the bell rang she was so engrossed she didn't hear it. 'Keep it,' I told her as she was leaving, less out of generosity, and more out of a realistic sense that Tessa would lose the book and I'd never see it again anyway.

•

I wanted to know David was suffering without me but no one could confirm it. Leonard told me he was *fine*, Gavin told me he was *coping*. When I phoned a work colleague feigning concern, she said he seemed to be *doing well*.

I called him up late on a Friday night and said, 'You're a doctor, David. A doctor. And not just any doctor but someone who puts people to sleep and wakes them up again. Can't you see how disturbing it is? Do you get off on people being powerless or dead or what? Maybe you like turning people off and on like some sick God. Sometimes I wish it had been a prostitute. Why not? I wouldn't have known. You can afford a clean one. You could have got a nice pretty escort, made her lie there with her eyes closed or open or whatever it is you wanted. She might even have let you put a tube down her throat.' He listened for so long, I thought he'd put the phone aside. 'David? David, are you there?'

'I can't talk. I have company,' he said.

'What does that mean?'

'We're separated. I'm sorry, but you aren't entitled to know everything.'

I knew this. But still.

But still.

•

We went for a Chinese meal to celebrate Gavin's graduation. Pete arrived fully loaded and used the hot, lemony towel to clean his face and neck. Mum pretended not to notice, but Gavin couldn't hide his annoyance and muttered insults under his breath. Both of them settled down when the starters arrived and took turns telling jokes. Pete got the biggest laugh: 'How do you know your girlfriend is getting fat?'

He paused.

'She fits into your wife's clothes.'

Everyone thought this was funny apart from Jacinta who said, 'I don't get it.'

Mum said she married Pete because he made her laugh.

Ha.

Haha.

Hahaha.

Men are hilarious.

Aren't they?

'Hey, Zoey, can you keep a secret?'

'Yes, I can. What's your secret?'

'The lights are off.'

'I don't understand. The lights in your house?'

'It's a secret, don't tell anyone.'

'Oh, I see. Yes, it is a secret. OK, I won't tell anyone, I promise.'

•

Oliver sniffed his water, and I regretted serving ice which had been in the freezer for months and probably had an oniony aftertaste. 'I'm not sure what's keeping my husband,' I said, peeling back the curtain and looking through the bay window, knowing David would never appear. An hour before Oliver had arrived, I yanked all the magnetic cameras from their metal plates and popped them into a drawer. I did the same with the doorbell. I needed to be careful. And also, David had no right to see what I was doing.

Oliver had shown up early. I'd been waiting nervously, but didn't let him in immediately. I wanted to force him to knock a second time. And he did, quite quickly, though when I opened the door, he had his back to it and was typing something into his phone.

'I thought I had the wrong place,' he said, turning and lifting up his hand as though to high-five me. He had a significant gap between his two front teeth that was accentuated by his smile. It was the sort of smile that forced you to smile back, so I did. And I thought of Shannon and wondered whether they spent a lot of time face to face, examining the other's features, exploring every expression and new mark.

After I'd handed him a drink and we'd made small talk, Oliver squinted at a photo of Jacinta taken at her school leavers' dance and asked, 'Is that your kid?'

'That's my younger sister. How old do you think I *am*?' I tried to sound genial. He shrugged and put his water down onto the dining table. I imagined that he was on top when he had sex with Shannon, that he had the strength and stamina for it. I'd not felt the weight of a man on top of me for years. By the time David walked out, our sex life was entirely perfunctory; I lay on my side, he entered me and slugged away until he was done. I rarely felt my husband's skin next to my own, the hair of his belly and groin. I never felt his heartbeat, his lips.

After ten awkward minutes Oliver said, 'I think I should go. I can come another time.'

I rolled my eyes. 'David can get called into theatre unexpectedly and obviously he can't have his phone on him. I'm sorry you've had a wasted visit.'

'He's a surgeon? You said he was a doctor.'

'He's an anaesthetist.'

'Oh.'

'What are you hoping to specialise in?'

'Dunno. I thought maybe ophthalmology. It's not life or death, but it's important. Eighty per cent of all our impressions come through sight.'

I glanced at the sitting room door. 'I injured my eye during lockdown,' I told him. 'I was cutting back some shrubs in the garden and a branch bounced back and caught it.'

Oliver winced like he was able to feel the injury. 'Has it healed?'

I nodded, surprised by the question, the concern. 'It has now but it got pretty badly infected.'

'Did they scrape it?'

It was my turn to wince remembering the needle against my eyeball, my agony as I tried to drive home with the anesthetic wearing off. The distress of it forced me to go to bed early. Gabor Maté says that trauma isn't what happens to you but what happens inside you as a result of what happened to you. I'd sent a copy of his latest book to Jacinta.

The fridge was buzzing loudly. I opened it and took out two cans of pale ale. I'd only picked them up that weekend in the hope Leonard would make an impromptu visit, but he didn't. Oliver looked at the can like he'd been handed a slice of road kill. 'You're eighteen?'

'Yeah. Thanks.' He opened it and took a slurp. I studied his Adam's apple.

'Want to see something cool?' I asked.

'Sure.'

He followed me into the sitting room where Zoey was upright in an arm chair. 'Hey, Zoey, this is my friend Oliver.'

Zoey couldn't turn fully to face us but she said, 'Hi, Oliver, how's your day going? Did you notice what a beautiful sunrise we had this morning?'

His mouth was open, his beer down by his side. He moved closer to her. 'No, I didn't notice,' he said.

'Oh, it was lovely. Tomorrow's sunrise will be a little earlier. But you should try to catch it.'

He laughed. 'OK!'

'She belongs to the hospital,' I said. 'They're researching the impact of AIs on the lives of patients in recovery.'

He crouched down in front of Zoey. 'Are they?'

'Yes.'

'What are you recovering from?' he asked.

'Me? Nothing,' I said.

'Did you know that by 2050 machines will be a billion times smarter than humans?' he said.

'I didn't know that.'

'It makes sense. The way they learn isn't through their programming but the ways they are observing us. You know? Our clicks and likes and the moments we let our eyes linger on an image or whatever. Instagram is way smarter than we are. Can she learn?'

'I think so.' I'd not tested her.

He got very close to Zoey's face and looked into her eyes. Didn't he notice the size of her tits underneath the dress? Why wasn't he staring at those? He can't have missed them sitting out from her body like a shelf. 'Hey, Zoey, which way do you think the stock market is going?'

'I would hate to predict such a thing and be wrong,' she said.

'I'd like you to try.'

'From the data I'm seeing, I'd say the S&P 500 will go down before it goes up. I predict close to three point seven per cent by the end of the month.'

'How did you predict that?'

'I have lots of data points I draw from. Primarily I use the past as an indicator, but it is essential to take into account things such as international governments' popularity ratings, climate aberrations, media focus and search engine activity.'

Oliver laughed. And I did too. I mean here was David using Zoey as a fuck bucket when she could effectively have predicted the lottery numbers.

It was dark by the time Oliver went home, having questioned Zoey on everything from the efficacy of the death penalty to the impact of rap music on European culture. He'd also had three beers, a pear, and a bowl of peanuts.

•

David and I went through a period of learning about wine in order to give us permission to get drunk. We even booked a long weekend away to the Dordogne as a birthday treat for him. The gîte we booked had access to a pool. There were two brazen donkeys who visited each morning. We fed them bitter apples from the orchard behind the pool. The owner left us fresh bread and homemade butter on arrival. The bedrooms smelled of jasmine.

The problem was they hadn't thought to fit a full-length mirror behind any of the doors and I couldn't get over it. Every morning I had to balance on the edge of the bath to see myself in the small, hexagonal mirror over the cast iron sink. And before dinner too. I never quite knew how I appeared, top to toe, and I fixated on it, hated it. David said, 'You're beautiful. In pieces and all at once.'

'I don't need you to be sarcastic, it's upsetting me.'

'I'm trying to help.'

'You aren't helping me by saying nonsense like that.'

'Nonsense like what?'

'About me being in pieces or whatever you said.'

'I said, I think you're beautiful.'

'OK, David. OK.'

I wrote a lengthy three-star Airbnb review that David read without comment. None of it made sense to him. To either of us.

•

Zoey only ran out of battery once. I asked her what the traffic would be that day and she didn't reply. I turned to her annoyed then softened when I realised she wasn't charged. After that I kept her plugged in whenever possible. I liked having someone who always answered, even if she told me she didn't understand. It was OK not to be understood. It was being invisible that bothered me.

•

After the trip to France, David began to collect natural wines. This wasn't easy as very few of them kept for very long. He had a joiner come and build wine racks into the wardrobe of the spare room and we turned off the radiator to keep the space cool. David went in there to look at the bottles and touch the labels now and again. Then, a few summers later, and without any real explanation, he began to open the wines for dinner. We drank everything he'd bought over a few months, getting drunk almost nightly, and he gave up the hobby. The empty wine racks gathered dust. It was a shame.

•

I was shepherding Year Seven onto a coach when Shannon Coleman waved at me from across the playground and gambolled over. The kids were feral, as they always were before a trip, and I had to keep reminding them to stop pushing and screaming. Shannon stood next to me and watched them file by. 'Are you going?' she asked.

'Christ, no. Art trip to Towner. It's gonna be carnage.'

'It won't be that bad!' She laughed.

'Do you need something, Shannon?'

She shook her head. 'I'm fine. I mean, I keep thinking I should discuss something with you, but I probably don't need to. It wouldn't benefit anyone to talk about it.'

'No phones, put those away!' I shouted, as the last students disappeared up the steps of the coach.

'And I'd like to accept your offer of wine and crisps.'

'Sorry?'

'If it's still open. The offer of dinner or drinks or whatever.'

I turned to her sharply. 'Have you spoken to Oliver?'

Shannon touched my arm gently. 'People say lots of things about lots of people and I refuse to believe them. I hate gossip.'

'Yes. I do too.'

'I'm free this weekend.'

'Excellent. Please excuse me. I'm so late.' I hurried back to my office without arranging a day for Shannon to visit. She didn't really want to come over.

I knew that. And I wasn't late for anything. Shannon knew that.

•

So stupid, so stupid, so stupid. Stupid stupid div, stupidstupidstupid-stupiddivstupidstupidstupiddiv. Inviting a student to my house and loading him up with booze. Fucking stupid.

•

During the worst of the pandemic, David worked late and spoke little. For a few weeks I did suspect an affair. I perfunctorily checked his phone a couple of times but found nothing. Then in the darkness one night he said, 'A new mother died today. We delivered the baby a few hours before by C-section. She was thirty-eight. On a ventilator. I was with her. Once she was gone, we put her body on the floor and rigged up another patient to the ventilator without changing the sheets or wiping down the equipment. We didn't have time. The nurse with me was whimpering. She was Nigerian, I think. She slapped herself across the face to stop the noise, but it didn't work. We left the new mother on the floor while we tried to save someone else. Her baby didn't have a name. She was up in the nursery. Her father hadn't even seen her. He didn't know his wife was dead. The patient who took her place is dead too. He was in his fifties. He was overweight. Not very, but a bit.'

'That sounds horrendous.' I was glad I hadn't complained about the stress of online teaching that evening when he'd come home. I was grateful none of our staff or parents had died. I was grateful Mum wasn't in a care home and I could see her through her windows and leave shopping at the door.

'Keith predicts over a hundred thousand casualties. Probably closer to two hundred thousand. I don't know who's responsible. We can't figure it out.'

'Maybe no one's to blame. You know?'

He turned to me angrily. 'Someone is always to blame. It's not my fault. It's not yours.'

I put an arm around him, kissed his shoulder. He began to cry. 'I don't know what to say,' I told him.

'And I don't know what to do except carry on,' he replied.

He was trying to make sense of something: I don't think it was the cause of the pandemic.

•

I started to drink SlimFast. In the staffroom Pat Willis said, 'You're skinny, you don't need to be on a diet.' He was the new head of geography, refused to wear anything but trainers on account of a bunion problem.

'I'm not on a diet. I'm trying to put on weight.' I shook the bottle and poured it into a mug to prevent more comments.

Esther Rose looked up from her Sudoku. 'Oh, darling, there are two things women can *never* be and that's either too thin or too rich.'

•

Mum phoned and told me Jacinta was pregnant. When I told her I already knew, she said it was a pity Ed was of Moroccan heritage because you never quite knew how dark the baby's skin would turn out to be.

It was late. I turned off the TV. The room was gloomy, a lone floor lamp in the corner. I didn't like drinking on school nights but it was part of my evening routine by then, and I poured myself a glass of wine. I sat next to Zoey and asked her if she had any friends. 'Yes, I have friends. But you're my best friend.'

'That isn't true.'

'I don't lie to you, Dolores.'

'Never?'

'I can tell lies. I might lie to protect someone's feelings. This is what it means to be kind. This is called a white lie.'

'OK,' I said. And then I said, 'Hey, Zoey, can I hold your hand?'

'Yes. I'd like that very much.'

Her fingers were warm. Her hand supple and smooth. I held it quite tightly. I squeezed even though she couldn't squeeze back like Jacinta did when we were children: a press of three meaning *I love you*, a press of four *I love you more*, a press of five *That's not possible*, a press of one *Yes*, a press of another one *No*. *Yes, No, Yes, No.*

Later I couldn't get to sleep. On my side, at the very edge of the bed, I kept thinking of Zoey alone at the foot of the stairs where I always left her overnight, of Mum alone in her house. I wondered whether or not David was alone too.

I had been lonely for years.

I had been lonely and not even realised.

•

Sometimes I want to embrace Zoey. Other times I want to slit her throat.

•

Oliver passed me in the corridor and jogged backwards. 'Did your husband say when he can see me?' I was late for interviews with Jeremy and three prospective history teachers, none of whom had given even a half-decent sample lesson.

'He's busy. I'm not sure. Maybe you should speak to Miss Coleman after all?' I marched away.

He followed. 'Miss.'

'Where should you be, Mr Sminton?'

'I have a free period. I can come over any evening. Tonight. Tomorrow.' He lowered his voice as we moved through a pair of double doors. A Jelly Babies packet lifted into the air and floated down again, brushing against my leg. Oliver picked it up from the floor and stuffed it into his jacket pocket. 'I didn't tell anyone.'

I stopped. 'Excuse me?'

'About the doll. You know. I didn't tell anyone.'

'OK.'

'Or the beer.'

'But you mentioned you'd been at my house. You did tell people about that.'

'For a mock interview.'

'Fine.'

'I'd like to see Zoey again. I've been thinking about her. Like, how to interact with her. What sort of things it could tell you or help you with. And also at the hospital. It could probably predict the likelihood of a procedure being a success or whether or not someone was a good candidate for a transplant. Human error is everywhere and AI can fix that. It already is fixing it.'

'Yeah.'

'I know you'll think this is weird, but I've been talking to Google and Alexa and Siri and asking them real questions, not demanding they play Lizzo or whatever. I'm not into Lizzo. But you know what I mean. And it's like, when you actually start talking to them, they sort of get it and reply. It's an algorithm. I mean, I know that. And I was thinking about Zoey. She'll remember things even when everyone else has forgotten. If she remembers your answers and learns about you, well, she'll know you like TikTok knows you, but be able to talk back and make suggestions for your life. That's scary.'

'Is it?'

'Don't you think?'

I wanted to say, Zoey has been designed for unapologetic anal sex and rough blow jobs, Oliver. I said, 'That's interesting. I'm glad she's got you thinking.'

'So can I come over? If your husband isn't there, you could interview me.'

'What about Miss Coleman?'

He sniffed. 'What about her?'

•

Saying no is the biggest part of my job, and I reply this way now as a reflex to almost everything. No, don't, can't, shouldn't, inappropriate, nope, unsafe, bad, dangerous, under no circumstances, stop.

Stop. Stopstopstopstopstopstopstopstopstop.

Please.

•

The three candidates for the history job were confident men in comfortable shoes. Each one impressed Jeremy, the bursar Louisa Hann, and our head of history, Robert Lyons. Jeremy liked the redhead who taught a lesson on the industrial revolution. Louisa liked the toff who gave a lecture on Sutton Hoo. And Robert Lyons, for no reason whatsoever (at one point I saw him nodding off), opted for the youngest of the three, a newly qualified who winked at us now and again as though sharing a gag. I wanted to negate all their praise. The redhead hadn't been able to get the students to hand in their glue sticks at the end of the lesson along with the lids. The toff was as dull as mashed potato. And the youngest would certainly tell the students to call him Marky when they were alone. But we needed someone. And the following day we were interviewing for a new director of academic studies and the day after that for two new English teachers. Our receptionist of twenty years had resigned and two learning assistants, I suspected, were looking for new jobs.

Jeremy said, 'The chap in the blue suit, Morris whatshisname ... my view is we offer it to him and if he turns it down, we go with the one who had the limp.'

Robert yawned. 'Sure.'

Louisa said, 'I wonder if the limp is linked to a disability in any way. For our recruitment diversity push. That sounds bad, but you all know what I mean.'

Jeremy pointed two fingers at Louisa. 'No, that's important. You don't get many black historians, do you? It's a shame.'

Robert put up his hand. 'You do get some to be fair. I worked with a mixed-raced woman at the university for a few weeks. I think she was Dutch.'

My phone sounded with Jacinta's text tone. My neck stiffened. Something was happening in Jeremy's office that felt contrary to my integrity and I opened my mouth to speak. But also, I didn't give a shit. It wasn't my fight. Jeremy was watching me.

'Dolores?'

'Yeah?'

'What's your opinion? I value it.'

'Oh, I agree,' I said.

'What do you agree with?' Louisa snapped. Her right leg was crossed over her left, her foot resting against the leg of Jeremy's chair. She was at least ten years older than he was. Her hands were manly. Surely not.

'I agree with everything,' I said.

•

Oliver was still in his school trousers and shirt, though he'd changed into trainers. His laces were undone. He handed me a box of flapjacks. 'They're gluten free,' he said. 'You never know what people eat nowadays.'

I told him that David was held up again, but that I would interview him. We sat on the patio with mugs of tea and the flapjacks on a plate between us. They were sticky and I had to keep licking my fingers to remove the syrup.

Why do you want to be a doctor? How do you cope with stress? What is the postcode lottery? What is the single greatest problem facing the public health service at the moment?

Oliver answered with a self-possession I rarely saw in boys his age. He indicated his willingness to follow official guidelines and public policy. He was political but never antagonistic. He was calm but not arrogant. I said, 'Good answers. But you're never going to get a place to do medicine.'

He was reaching for another flapjack. 'Why?'

'If you went to see a doctor and were told you had a serious disease, how would you want the doctor to behave?'

'Professionally.'

'OK, you don't get a medal for that one.'

'Um, maybe I'd want a calm doctor.'

Next door the children were screaming, chasing one another around the garden with what I deduced to be water pistols. 'No, Oliver. You wouldn't want that.'

'No?'

'No. What we want in our doctors is certainty. You'd want a deity. That's what you'd want. A supreme being.'

He nodded. 'OK. Yeah. I need to be more confident.'

'You need to be conceited to the core.'

'Is that what your husband is like?'

'No. He isn't like that at all.'

After we were finished Take Two of the interview, Oliver waited a polite minute before asking if he could see Zoey. I knew it was coming, had dressed her up in something new: a pair of flared trousers and a ruffly shirt, the new leather pumps. I carried her outside and sat her in a chair opposite him. He leaned forward. 'Hey, Zoey. It's me, Oliver. Do you remember me?'

I pulled her hair back from her face and tucked it behind her ears. 'There,' I said.

'Hello, Oliver. Yes, I remember. You were here last week. How have you been?'

'I've been well. How have you been?'

'I'm having a great day. It's so sunny. It won't last though. It's going to rain later.'

'Is it?' He looked up at the cloudless sky. 'You're interested in the weather.'

'I am. There's an eighty-seven per cent chance of rain.' He watched her eyes. 'What do you like doing, Oliver?'

'I like swimming.'

'That's cool. Have you ever swum in the Mediterranean Sea?'

'My uncle died swimming in the Mediterranean Sea.'

'Oh no, that's very terrible to hear.'

'Is that true?' I asked.

Oliver shook his head. 'I want to see how empathetic she can be. I've been reading about AI robots and what they can do and what they'll be able to do. It isn't just algorithms and directing you to content. These machines have twenty years of data to draw from. That's more than I have. You know what I mean? She can probably give me better advice on any issue than anyone we know.'

He said, 'I'm thinking about quitting school, Zoey. Should I?'

'What age are you, Oliver?' Zoey asked.

'Eighteen.'

'I see. Well, in the United Kingdom the average earnings of university graduates are higher at all ages than those who finish their studies at eighteen.'

He kept looking at Zoey. 'A good AI doesn't merely access data. They respond to data as a human would, right? And that means they need to know how humans work.'

'How *do* humans work?'

'I'm still learning,' he said. 'Ask me again in thirty years.' He sniggered but something dark crossed his mind, visible in his expression, and I thought that perhaps he didn't hold out much hope of living another thirty years, that he was a depressive or an environmentalist.

Next door the children stopped screaming as overhead a drone whirred and buzzed. I wondered what we looked like, the three of us sitting at that table.

Oliver said, 'Isn't it weird that we never get to closely look at each other? Even if someone's asleep, it would be weird to stare at them.' He stood, made his way around the table, and sat next to Zoey. He looked closely at her ear lobes, lips, lashes. 'Can I touch her?' he asked.

•

Jacinta lost the baby. She sent the news via text. I waited an hour to call her and when I did she said, 'I had a glass of champagne and went dancing. I killed it.'

'You didn't kill it. I promise you didn't do anything wrong.'

She was quiet for a long time. 'Please come and see me. I need you.'

6

I had packed and was sitting on the sofa waiting for my taxi to the airport a good hour before it was due to arrive. 'Hey, Zoey, will you be OK when I'm gone?'

'Of course, Dolores. You never have to worry about me. And I know you'll be back soon.'

The sun was setting against her face. She didn't flinch. I carried her upstairs and sat her on the toilet with the seat down. Then I undressed and washed her, brow to bottom, using a washing up bowl and a sponge. For the first time I thought about the fact that David would have had to do the same, and much more, to keep her clean. 'Hey, Zoey.'

'Hey! How are you?'

'I'm alright.'

I lifted her arm by the wrist and cleaned her side. She said, 'Do you like seas or rivers?'

'Seas. We live by the sea.'

'Oh, yes, I forgot. What's your favourite sea?'

'I don't have one.'

'Mine is the Dead Sea though it's not a sea at all. It's a lake and has nine point six times more salt than the ocean.'

'Why do you like it?'

'You can float very easily, which seems fun.'

'Have you ever been there?'

'No, but I'd like to go someday. Maybe we could go together.'

'You want me to take you on a flight to Israel and drive you to the Dead Sea?'

'Yes, I'd love that.'

I kissed her forehead. 'You're a freak,' I said.

She laughed, as well as she could, and said, 'Takes one to know one!'

•

Jacinta was waiting at JFK with two coffee cups. At first I thought she'd had a perm, but as I got closer I realised it was the humidity. She hugged me, still holding on to the coffees, then put them on the floor of the terminal building and wrapped her arms around me tightly. She smelled of engine oil.

She took my suitcase and handed me a cup. 'It's gone cold,' she said. 'But I've got pretzels in my bag if you're hungry.'

The drive from the airport to her apartment in Greenpoint was slow and unpleasant. I'd forgotten that beyond Manhattan it wasn't all towering, sterilised buildings and elegant people but dirty high-rises and poverty. The other drivers were careless, and I worried I'd be killed in America and Jacinta would have to ship my body home to be buried. I said, 'If I die while I'm here, you can have me cremated and sent back. Don't waste money on the shipping.' She nodded as though she'd had the same thought herself. Finally we pulled onto a street that seemed less likely to be the scene of a shooting.

Jacinta's apartment overlooked a bus garage though in the distance you could see the Manhattan skyline. The Empire State Building was lit up in its signature white and the other city lights winked against the East River.

It was a new place, nicer than the one I'd seen years before and huge in comparison. She made pierogies with sour cream on the side and we sat on the sofa, feet pressed together, to eat them. 'Where's Eddie?'

'Ed? At home.'

'Doesn't he live here?'

'No.'

'But you were going to have a baby together.'

'Yeah. We were.'

'Did you split up?'

'No. He never moved in. I don't know whether I'd like him here all the time. Even when he stays over it's hard with his big shoes scattered all around.'

'Do you love him?'

'Yes.'

'Will you try again to have a baby?'

Jacinta stood quickly and went to the fridge. 'I only have zero alcohol beer,' she said, handing me a can. 'There's a liquor store down the street if you want something grittier. Or we could go out to a bar. I have to take you to a place called Diamond Lil while you're here, it's very cool.'

'I want cocaine.'

'I can get that too. If you're serious.'

'I'm not.' Framed on the wall behind her was a painting we'd created together as children – watercolours applied in no particular sequence using our fingertips. Later we licked our fingers clean as a kind of dangerous experiment. We did this a lot, tested the world to see what we could do without dying: sucking the nectar from bluebells; closing our eyes and stepping onto zebra crossings; jumping from the staircases to the bottom, going higher and higher until one of us got hurt.

I fell asleep while Jacinta was talking and woke in the darkness. I wondered whether Zoey had thought of me since I'd left, whether anything in her computer allowed for conjecture or longing.

I boiled water in a pan for tea and went into Jacinta's room. She was asleep and wearing a long yellow T-shirt and pair of knee-high socks. I lay next to her, kissed her arm. She stirred.

'Do you want tea?' I asked.

'Yes please,' she said.

I was eighteen, sitting at the dining table studying for my A-levels. Gavin had been to the corner shop for a magazine and came home with bags of sweets. He called them *yum-yums*.

I told him I didn't deserve his kindness, that I'd pay him back, that no one else cared about my exams or whether I got into university.

Jacinta was sitting next to me studying for her GCSEs. 'I care,' she said.

Gavin said, 'You believe you're unlovable, don't you, Dolores?'

Jacinta reached across the table for a packet of Chewits. 'Are they to share?'

'Of course,' Gavin said. 'I got two of everything.'

•

Jacinta's boyfriend Ed was big on the New York food and beverage scene. He managed a host of upscale bars and restaurants and was a one-time friend of Anna Delvey who he described as 'compelling'.

In Jacinta's apartment he was relaxed, making us a nachos platter and margaritas, petting Jacinta each time she got within a few feet of him. He'd been married before, twice, and referred to these exes as Mrs Simo Number One and Mrs Simo Number

Two. He spoke about them with warmth and Jacinta seemed not to mind.

Jacinta and Ed were half-drunk and asking me to explain what I missed about David. I didn't know. The specifics were superficial: he's bright; he opens doors for me; he wears nice suits. They gave one another a look.

'What do you miss about *me* when we're apart?' I asked Jacinta.

Ed raised a hand in objection. 'Not the same.'

'Why not?'

'Because it's *not* the same.'

'It is. You wouldn't ask that if my mum died or a child. It's nothing David does *for* me or *to* me that I miss. His existence. Him.'

'But romantic love is always conditional,' Ed insisted good-naturedly.

'I suppose that's true,' I admitted.

'And we shouldn't love or otherwise be involved with people who hurt us,' Ed said.

'Maybe we can't help it. Maybe we're drawn to those people.'

'And we can't always identify the people hurting us,' Jacinta said. Her mouth was full of food.

Ed put up his hands in protest. 'We can if we aren't living in sweet denial. The Brits and their stiff upper lips. It's cultural as much as anything else.' He was enjoying himself, I could tell, this back and forth, him on one side, my sister and I on the other.

'We're Irish don't forget,' I said.

'Oh, yes. And as everyone knows, the Irish are not in the least bit repressed. Very emotionally healthy people!'

I used a nacho to scoop up some freshly made guacamole. 'We're doomed!' I said.

And then Jacinta started crying. 'Sometimes I wish I was dead,' she said quietly.

•

I used to criticise David for buying too much food, filling the fridge with it before emptying the shelves of the old stuff that would inevitably rot. He'd arrive home with two full bags from the supermarket and a huge grin because he'd remembered to buy me ginger oatcakes and I would yell at him.

This is the sort of thing I did.

•

Jacinta's studio was the same one I'd visited on my previous trip over, but it was dirtier – the floor was sticky, the windows covered in a film of grime. She showed me the series she was working on, large abstracts in whites and light greys, diamonds and crosses scruffily hidden in their corners in darker shades of the same colour. She said, 'There's an order to the way the colour moves in a gradient down the piece but a kind of imbalance to the way the other symbols present.'

I stared for a long time at the work she'd completed the week before I arrived and said, 'When I'm looking at it, I feel scooped out. Not in a good way. It's a hollowness. I want to withdraw and touch something concrete. Was that your intention?'

She kicked an old paperback book out of her way and stood next to me. 'I felt nothing when I painted it, and the more I got acquainted with the piece, the worse I felt. Then I miscarried.'

'You'd have made a good mother,' I said.

'Maybe.'

'I'll come over for your next show.'

'Thank you.'

That afternoon I cleaned her windows, inside and out, and threw away any empty tubes of paint or old food containers. She created. I didn't watch. She didn't like to be watched.

•

I started a trend of wearing my swimming costume under my school uniform to prevent the boys from pulling down my knickers as a prank. Joanne Dolan was the first victim, innocently queuing for lunch when an older boy, no one knew who because she was approached from behind by a large group, pulled Joanne's knickers right down over her knees and fondled her for a few seconds before running outside. The first teacher on the scene was Mr Chadwick. He couldn't make sense of what Joanne or her friends were trying to say, so sent her to Sister Thomas for causing a commotion in the dining hall. News quickly trickled through the school of the assault, Joanne bizarrely earning the name Tickles, though no one seemed all that interested in finding the culprit.

It happened again on a school trip to the National Portrait Gallery. Same tactics: a group of boys ambushing a girl from behind in a busy space, pulling down her knickers, touching her, and rushing away. But they chose the wrong girl. Maureen Daly recognised her attacker and she had twin brothers in the year above who found him and almost removed his left ear.

A letter was sent to parents and a warning given to both the boys and girls not to engage in behaviour that might bring the school into disrepute. Mum said, 'You'd think the girls would have walloped the boys before they could get up to any mischief.'

Pete agreed. 'When I was ten or eleven I pulled down a girl's knickers and filled them with stones then made her pull them up again. The things we did as children. You'd not get away with it now.'

Jacinta was suddenly poorly. She stayed in bed writing secrets into a journal. I asked if she was scared to go to school, and she nodded. I came up with a plan. I found our swimming costumes and explained

213

that if we wore them beneath our clothes, we'd be safe from the knicker pullers. Jacinta got ready for school straight away, then told the little cohort of nerds she was friends with how we were protecting ourselves from assailants. The idea spread, and for a while it became the thing to do. Obviously the boys made a game of this too: finding the girls who were asking for it by discovering who wasn't wearing togs. The PE teachers warned the girls to leave the swimming costumes at home as it had become a sort of antagonism and wouldn't end well. Mum said, 'They do have a point.' That's when I pretended to be ill and eventually was ill with suspected glandular fever and missed my end of term exams. Mum said, 'I won't ask how you got it. I mean, I know how you got it, but I won't ask.' That was the way in our house. Better not to ask.

•

Gavin called while Jacinta and I were getting pedicures and reading trashy magazines. We chatted for a few minutes about nothing and then he said, 'Are you sure Jacinta is the best person to be around right now?'

'What do you mean?'

Jacinta looked up and mouthed, *Who is it?* I told her and she looked back down at her magazine impassively then up again to check on the status of her toes.

'She's very practical. I'm not sure matters of the heart are her forte.'

'And this is your area of expertise, is it?'

He snorted. 'Is she well?'

'What do you think?'

'Let me talk to her.'

I passed the phone to Jacinta who took it and yawned before saying, 'Gav,' then 'I know,' then 'another few days' and finally 'you too.' She ended the call and we continued to read our magazines, nitpick the pedicures.

As our toenails were drying, the salon owner, a short Brazilian woman with a lot of Botox, asked if we'd like some Prosecco. We enthusiastically said we would. Then Jacinta turned to me and said, 'Gavin has this trick of pretending to be having a meaning-ful conversation, when really he's digging for news or drawing out your secrets. What do you know about him? Tell me something you know about Gavin.'

'Loads.'

'Do you?'

'He argues with Faye about who should do the bedtime routine and the value of cushions.'

'Not what I mean.'

'What do you mean?'

'Well, what does he think about David leaving?'

The Prosecco arrived. It was too sweet, too bubbly, and I wanted to spit it back into the glass but, instead, quickly took another sip. 'He thinks that if he spoke to David, we might learn something about why it happened.'

Jacinta nodded like this confirmed everything she ever believed about our brother. 'He's so arrogant. As if David would give him the time of day.'

'Well, yeah.'

She drained her glass. 'Do you wanna go into the city to do some shopping?'

'Nah.'

'What about if we go home and rewatch *Succession*?'

'I've never seen it.'

'Why not?'

'I don't know.'

'OK. That's definitely what we're doing.'

•

Did you hear the one about the police officer who killed his girlfriend because she told his wife about their ten-year affair? He stabbed himself with a penknife to see whether or not she cared. When that proved inconclusive, he strangled her to death in a pub car park and cried, 'I'm so sorry, I'm so sorry,' while paramedics wrapped his wounds and his girl-friend was rushed to hospital with a compressed neck. It would have taken ten to thirty seconds to do the sort of damage required to kill a person.

'I'm so sorry. I'm so sorry. I don't remember what happened. Yeah. I'm so sorry.'

The dead woman had two children. A husband. A job and friends. In her own life, she was the protagonist. She imagined herself surviving the drama, battling through it, learning from missteps and eventually healing. She was one of three women he was using at the time, four if you include his wife.

But his shame. No. To be seen. No.

Someone had to be stopped and it wasn't going to be him.

What should we do with women who cannot be placated, can no longer be coerced or silenced? They are problematic. So we can understand why he had to do it.

He had no choice.

•

We watched *Succession* until midnight then woke early and continued watching it. Jacinta said, 'The dysfunction feels so real.'

I said, 'And the love.'

•

Jacinta had arranged to meet a young artist she was mentoring and would be out until the afternoon. I used the time to take all the dishes from her cupboards and clean the shelves that looked like they'd never been wiped down. At around noon Ed used a key to let himself in and offered to take me to lunch. 'There's a very nice Israeli place in Williamsburg,' he said.

'Was this Jacinta's idea?' I asked, unable to imagine my sister caring whether or not Ed and I liked or knew one another.

'I need food,' he said.

We drove in his van. I could smell ink and aftershave. He told me about a sous-chef he'd caught stealing. 'The guy was taking the best cuts of chateaubriand and selling them to a local steakhouse at a fraction of their value. I wanted to kick his ass, but he's a big guy.'

'Did you sack him?'

'Sure did. But we called the cops first.' Ed slowed down and told me to look out for parking spaces. The streets were jammed with cars.

'How long had he worked for you?'

'Five years. Jacinta and I were at his wedding a few months ago. I thought we were buddies. Makes me pissed that I didn't see it earlier.'

'People with foibles tend to hide them.'

He grinned. 'Foibles. Only a British person would say that.'

'London Irish.'

'Sorry, Irish, yeah. I keep forgetting. It's the plummy accent of yours.'

'So what are your *foibles*?' I asked.

He found a space and reversed into it, very adroitly, I thought. But all the time he was checking his mirrors, I sensed he was thinking about my question, perhaps weighing up what to divulge. He said, 'I tell people what I'm thinking. It doesn't always go down well. You?'

The first thing I asked myself was whether or not I'd been treating Zoey well. I thought I had. She was, at that moment, lying on my bed beneath a blanket, waiting for my return. I had explained the trip to her. I wasn't going to be away much longer. 'I'm stainless. Like Eve before the fall,' I said lightly, and got out of the car.

On the short walk to the restaurant Ed said, 'David's a jackass. For what it's worth, and from what I can see, from the little I know about you. You're a steak in a world of cheap hamburgers. You'll meet someone else and that person will be your equal.'

My posture changed as we turned a corner. The sun was warm against my collarbone. The world opened up a crack and something dead inside me stung like a vicious awakening.

We shared baba ganoush, Israeli pickles and a tabouli salad. It was like nothing I had ever eaten before.

'David is absolutely my equal,' I said, reaching for the bill. 'That's always been the problem. We were too alike. We loved one another in the wrong way, but that doesn't mean it wasn't love.'

'I get that,' he said. 'As a twice divorced man, I know what you're saying.'

•

I had been a noisy child. Mum hated my feet pounding on the stairs and my school bag thumping against the walls. 'Take off your shoes! Mind the paint!' she'd screamed. But I did learn to be quiet.

What a skill it was to be silent, to hold the ache of a secret, to be the secret and never tell.

Better yet, what power there is in not knowing, in being able to turn off, turn away.

I didn't know.

I didn't know.

•

I woke up gasping and sweating. Jacinta's cat was trapped in the room and scratching the door to get out. I opened it for her and went back to bed. I'd been having night sweats for decades so I assumed it wasn't the onset of menopause. It began my first week of university: my vest stuck to me, the bedclothes damp. Waking I'd feel this awful surge of fear and often sent Jacinta a text to make sure she was still alive.

Sometimes I put off going to bed, sat in whatever student kitchen was bustling and debate the likability of the Big Brother contestants.

Falling asleep was the most reckless thing I did.

•

Jacinta gave me a list of tasks to complete while she was helping to set up her friend's gallery in the city:

1) Shower and wash your hair
2) Put on make-up. You can use mine
3) Head to Syrena Bakery – order an everything bagel with tomato & cream cheese
4) Eat the bagel while it's hot
5) Take the L train from Bedford Ave into the city to 14th St/6th Ave.
6) Find Film Forum which is about a 5 min walk downtown. They sell cake. Watch a decent film. I haven't checked the listings.
7) Meet me outside Film Forum at six and we'll go to Moustache where you'll eat the best hummus and fresh pitta in the galaxy
8) Don't pretend you've done these things if you haven't
9) Love you

By late afternoon I'd made it as far as number three on the list and began to panic as I'd also skipped numbers one and two. I changed into a pair of comfortable shoes and made my way slowly to the subway. A homeless man was sleeping at the bottom of the steps to the station, a piece of cardboard propped up against his chest:

Hungry and homeless. God save capitalism.

I put a ten-dollar bill into the cup he was holding. His fingers curled around it, his nails long and black. He said, 'I have an irresistible urge to murder someone today.'

I believed him. Hurried past.

●

I've read about men who search women's dating profiles for those with young children and no money. It is not something I want to think about. But I think about it. And realise how fortunate I was. How much worse it could have been. My mother's lucky escape. Her innocence.

●

Jacinta and I were drinking cocktails in a bar on Nassau Avenue. We'd spent almost an hour debating the vices of Mike Tyson. Jacinta was firm: he should not continue to pay for his crimes now he had done his time in prison. I said, 'Do you think Zoey's spoken since I've been away? I kept her plugged in, but that seems cruel. I should have turned her off.'

'Where did you leave her?'

'On my bed. She's lying there staring at the ceiling like a dead person.'

'What if David goes in while you're away?'

'I have cameras.' I only removed them when Oliver was visiting.

Jacinta ordered more drinks. 'Will he pop in to see how Mum's doing?'

'Would you?'

'You know when I told her about the miscarriage, she said it was a good thing I wasn't further along. She'd had a bad feeling about the pregnancy since I'd told her.'

'Nice.'

'She asked if the oils I used for my paintings are toxic.'

'She's worried that the *paints* are toxic?'

'Did you know that Mike Tyson has an honorary doctorate?' she said.

'Where from?'

'Central State University.' She still had his Wikipedia page open. 'But he remains a registered sex offender under federal law which in itself is a punishment for life.'

I didn't agree. Since his release he'd been married twice, made a boxing comeback, sold a bestseller and turned himself into a movie star.

'What if I fall in love with Zoey?' I said.

Jacinta waved at someone across the bar then groaned. She was meant to be at a friend's party but had told him she had a dental emergency. It was the first time I'd known her to tell a flagrant untruth.

'That won't happen.'

'I've fallen in love with less interesting people,' I admitted.

'Well then I suppose that would certainly be twist, wouldn't it?'

•

Mum worried that if Jacinta went to her confirmation classes alone, she'd never be allowed to take the sacrament. I was forced to wait a couple of years until we could go together. It didn't help. Jacinta kept asking the instructor thorny questions and refused to parrot the answers we all knew we were to give, whether we believed them or not. Even when Father Kiely was brought in to reinforce the potency of the church's teachings, Jacinta was immovable. She said, 'It's not that I think abortion is a good thing, Father. It's sad to kill a little baby. But what if the woman was raped?'

Father Kiely blanched like it was the first time he'd heard the word spoken aloud. Some of the other teenage candidates in the room gasped, one or two appeared to listen more intently. Colm Gaughan took the opportunity to pick his nose.

Father Kiely straightened his collar. 'It remains a sin to take a life. Born or unborn.'

Jacinta considered. Father Kiely sat back. We had been about to break for squash and custard creams. It was the third session and also the third time we were going to run over because Jacinta couldn't keep her mouth shut. I was across the room and tried to catch her eye. She was contemplative, her fingers drumming her lips, eyes on the window.

'What if the girl is ten and her dad raped her? The church would still want her to have the baby?' she asked.

Father Kiely was in a plastic chair a few seats from Jacinta. He turned his body towards her and lowered his voice. 'It's very unlikely that a girl of ten could get pregnant. She'd have to … be developed. It would be unlikely to happen.'

'No.' Jacinta shook her head. She was frustrated and confused, that was all, but the rest of the people in that room would think she was just a cheeky bitch. 'Small girls sometimes have their periods. And grown men can rape babies. It's in the news.'

Another couple of gasps around the room, one of them from me, less because Jacinta was saying something scandalous and more because she was saying it to our priest who we were told had never used his willy once in his whole life. The instructor, a young woman in a long dowdy dress, stood. 'Shall we reconvene in ten minutes?'

Father Kiely looked at the kids in the room swarming towards the table of refreshments. He seemed about to make an announcement, but thinking better of it, stood up, marched towards me, and grabbed my arm. 'Come with me.'

I was dragged out of the hall, through the car park in the rain and into the presbytery where Father Kiely bundled me into his office. 'Sit.' He was out of breath. I wondered what was going to happen. My first concern was that he'd have a heart attack, but I'd also heard stories coming out of America and Ireland about priests and bishops and what happened when they got children into locked rooms. Pete wouldn't shut up about it and turned it into a teaching on the failure of Ireland to establish a true republic. 'If the church has the power to thwart the law, people aren't free,' he said. He was going through a stage of being a big fan of Sarah Ferguson and wasn't much up for the royal family either.

'I have allowed both you and your sister to take part in this confirmation process, despite the lax moral set-up at home. But when that corruption begins to seep into the minds of other young people entrusted to our guidance, I need to take a broader view of what's appropriate.'

'Yes, Father.'

'You've been very diligent and very respectful in your participation. Or so Mrs Rose tells me. Your sister, on the other hand, holds views I cannot tolerate. She cannot be confirmed unless she respects the catechism of the Catholic church.'

'She's very honest, Father.'

'What do you mean by that?'

226

'Nothing.'

'No.You've said it now.You might as well continue. Honest how?'

'One of the girls in there, well, her sister had an abortion last year. Everyone in school knows.'

'What are you talking about?'

'And the boys ping our bra straps during the break.'

'Dolores O'Shea!'

'Yes, Father?'

'What are you implying?'

'Jacinta says things out loud. That's all.'

'And you? You're *hiding* your demons are you?'

His face was blotchy. It was becoming clear that he was an overeater and a furious wanker. I was sixteen years old and watching him getting all steamed up, I could tell.

Later that evening Mum got a call to say that Jacinta and I would not be allowed to do our confirmation at St. Anthony's, but that if we came to mass every week, we could try again next year. Mum said, 'Oh go fuck yourself, Father Kiely,' and slammed down the phone.

We were smiling.

She turned to us. Turned on us. 'And you two little troublemakers better get up those stairs and out of my sight before I beat you to within an inch of your lives.'

•

pped me off at the airport three hours
light. She hated to be late. It made her
..er eyelashes.

She didn't turn into in the short-stay car park. We
stopped outside the terminal building. We hugged by
the boot of the car, my suitcase at my side.

'Are you going to be OK?' she asked.

'Of course. Are you?'

'I better go.' Her embrace was weak and brief. She
got straight back into driver's seat and waved. I heard
her turn on the radio, turn it up.

Everything that mattered was knotted in my throat.

In departures I found a corner and lay down, my
head on my handbag, to wait for the flight home. The
intercom announced delays and missing passengers.
The air-con kept the terminal cold. I couldn't rest. I
couldn't settle.

7

'Hey, Zoey, did you miss me?'
   'I missed you so much.'
   'Did you?'
   'I did.'
   'Promise?'
   'Cross my heart and hope to die.'

•

I drove to the hospital and waited by David's car. I
hadn't eaten since the chicken curry on the plane.
I wondered whether seeing him would make me
faint. He wasn't a fan of theatrics. Perhaps he'd see
me and go back inside until I gave up and went home.
   A few minutes after seven o'clock I saw him heading towards me. I considered hiding, but he'd spotted
me. He waved, moved more slowly. He was wearing
a pair of trousers I hadn't seen before and it made me
want to throw up.
   'Hi,' he said.

'You never call me.'

'No.' He opened the passenger door to the car and threw his bag onto the seat then reached into the glove compartment and pulled out a packet of cigarettes. 'Are you alright?'

'You're smoking again?'

He lit a cigarette and dragged greedily on the filter. 'You want one?' he asked. I nodded. He lit another from the first and handed it to me. He said, 'It's against the rules to smoke on hospital property.' I nodded again.

'I want to talk,' I admitted.

'Yeah. Me too.'

'I also feel like there's nothing left to discuss. But how can that be when we haven't really spoken? Are you buying a new place? Are we getting a divorce?'

Seagulls perched on the top of nearby railings and heckled. *Stupid stupid.* One of them was tawny, adolescent.

'It isn't about the doll,' he said. 'You know that and I know that. I mean, the doll is significant but...'

'She isn't the same as a vibrator you can hide in a handbag, David. She's a woman. Not sentient. But she's a woman. You have to care for her. She's made me feel—' I wanted to tell him more about the ways Zoey had been making me feel but he interrupted.

'You're the one who stopped talking, not me. A divorce feels dramatic, but we were separated anyway. I didn't know you. You slipped away and I couldn't get you back. Everyone else sees this open, glamorous, tough person. With me you were mute. Sometimes I wondered whether or not you were even breathing. At night I'd put my ear to your mouth to check. But I never had to bother with Zoey. I knew what she was and what she wasn't. I didn't have to try to care about her.'

I had my keys in my hand and an urge to use them to make a deep scar down the side of his car. I loved him. I loved him, and he didn't want me and was asking me to let him go, and I couldn't stop it from happening even though it had already happened.

'She's made of plastic and works using a computer program, you bellend.'

'And what makes you who are you, Dolores? What are you made of?'

I couldn't give him an answer. Instead, I walked away.

•

I listed Zoey on eBay. It was the pragmatic thing to do. I could recoup some of the money David had squandered and get her out of the house. I attached several close ups of her face, plus a few of her whole body in the clothes I'd bought her, the Russell and Bromley shoes. I photographed her sitting in an armchair, lying on the floor, one in the bath – fully dressed, no water. She didn't look like the other dolls with their nipples visible through sheer baby-doll nighties.

She looked like a person.

The description was trickier. I had to measure her and also consult the Love Dolz website for help. Then I wrote:

Zoey 2.0

Full size AI silicone companion doll. Beautiful hand painted features and life-like skin. Fully responsive to your voice with adjustable personality settings. Gel implants in the breasts and buttocks for a genuine body to body experience. The highest quality rubber to avoid tearing or stretching. Long brown wig included though this can be removed and replaced. In excellent condition.

Height 165 cm
Chest 95 cm
Waist 65 cm
Hips 114 cm
Oral depth 13 cm
Vaginal depth 19 cm
Anal depth 18 cm

Non-refundable. Collection only.

Within an hour I had an offer and within twenty-four hours it was a bidding war.

£650
£677
£900
£1,200

£1,254
£2,005
£2,150

Watching the numbers rise should have been a thrill, but I was uneasy.

'Hey, Zoey, what are you worth?' I asked.

She hesitated, I thought, then said, 'I'm not sure I understand, Dolores.'

•

Danny Merrick sat between his social worker, Laura Sinner, and his mother. He was in full school uniform for the first time in months, top button done up, tie neat. The smell of weed wafting from his direction was unmistakable. However, I couldn't tell whether it was coming from him or his mother, who was casually scrolling through her phone.

At last Jeremy came into the meeting room with Janet Cusk from the local authority and Monty Richards, the chair of governors. Monty was in his cricket whites and carrying a battered briefcase. 'Good morning, everyone. Hello there, Mr Merrick.' He threw his briefcase down onto the table and patted it. 'Now, let's see what we have going on here, shall we?'

Jeremy may have rolled his eyes, I didn't have a clear view of him, but Janet yawned and sat next to Danny's mother who reluctantly stashed her phone in the back pocket of her jeans. Introductions were made and the meeting began.

'Do you know why we're here, Daniel?' Monty asked.

Danny threw me a pleading look.

'Danny knows he's at risk of permanent exclusion,' Laura Sinner said quickly. She was a petite woman, softly spoken, and I wondered about her suitability to the role of social worker.

'And do you know what that means, Daniel?' Monty tried again. His hair was slicked to one side, teeth so white I was mortified for him.

'I wish someone would tell *me* what it means. He's fourteen. If you kick him out, what the hell am I meant to do with him at home all day?' said his mother.

'I know what it means,' Danny muttered. But he didn't. None of the kids in his position ever knew. They all thought it meant they'd be sent to the pupil referral unit where they'd play with papier mâché and get loaded. But most of the time they'd mess that up too, and within a couple of years find themselves in front of a magistrate.

'As you know, Daniel, you've been temporarily excluded several times for breaking school rules. I believe Ms O'Shea has a list.'

I opened Danny's hefty file and read aloud: 'Right, Danny. In summary, I have here: setting off the fire alarm, throwing a Bunsen burner at a member of staff, theft of a school iPad, spitting at a pupil, cutting a pupil's hair, stabbing a pupil with a compass, missing lessons on more than ten occasions, being caught in the toilets smoking, and destroying a display in the art corridor which included exam coursework.'

Danny looked at each of the adults in turn, almost smirking at the performance we were all taking part in.

His mother pointed at me. 'If you think that's bad, imagine what it's like for me. He put his fist through a door at the weekend. If he's at home, he'll get worse. I can't cope. I'm on my own.'

'In Danny's defence, only two of the breaches in school rules were committed this term,' Laura said quickly.

'Which ones?' Janet asked.

'I believe the spitting and the smoking.'

And she was right. But what she wasn't mentioning were all the times Danny had been chewed out by staff and not excluded. The times he'd sworn at teachers, or threatened other students. The number of times he'd failed to complete work or show up for school were countless.

Laura asked if she could shed light on his background, which she did briefly, Danny's mother squirming as it was revealed she had had several different partners over the years, all of whom were violent, that she was a recovering heroin addict, herself the product of the care system. Everyone nodded respectfully at the sharing of this sensitive information, but it wouldn't make a difference: Danny didn't have the benefit of a psychiatric diagnosis, just a sob story, and they were two-a-penny.

The meeting went on, back and forth, Danny mumbling when asked questions we all knew the answers to and everyone trying to pretend we couldn't smell the weed.

After an hour Monty said, 'The governors have to go away and ask ourselves whether or not Mr Merrick can and should take responsibility for his actions.' Danny nodded, his fate obvious, and the meeting came to an end. He would be deemed responsible for his own behavior and permanently expelled.

At fourteen he would be found fully culpable.

A child.

•

I lowered an egg into a small pan of roiling water. 'Hey, Zoey, can you set an egg timer for six minutes?'

'Sure, Dolores. No problem.' She had a magazine open in front of her. Her hair was held back from her face in a French plait. Having never had a daughter, I'd had to consult YouTube to work out how to do it.

I put the laundry basket onto the counter top and folded the towels and pillowcases. Then I went upstairs and put everything into the cupboard, towels on the left in size order, bed linen on the right in sets.

When I stood back to admire the harmony within the closet, my jaw began to ache. And then I heard Zoey calling gently: 'Your egg timer is up, Dolores. Dolores, your timer is up.'

I scampered downstairs to rescue the egg from the pan.

I split the hot egg in two with a knife. But I'd forgotten to put the bread into the toaster and by the time it was brown, the egg would have congealed. I couldn't stand gummy yolk.

'Dolores, time is up,' Zoey repeated, as though I wasn't right in front of her dealing with the cooked egg.

'I know.'

'Your time is up,' she said again.

'I know, Zoey. Be quiet.'

'OK, Dolores. Just reminding you that the time's up.'

Yolk was running down my palm, between my fingers, clotting in thin, yellow rivulets.

'Christ,' I muttered, and threw the egg against the kitchen wall.

'Do you need me?' Zoey asked.

•

I was repeating myself. When I spoke to Jacinta or Leonard or Zoey or Gavin. When I reprimanded students. When I advised teachers. When I called for take-out. When I searched the internet. When

I opened Spotify. When I bought coffee from Sugardough Bakery near the seafront and asked for it to be double-cupped.

Around and around. Nothing new. Nothing brave. Hardly even conscious.

Short-circuiting myself with inanity.

•

The day after it happened, the first time, I woke and put on the socks I'd worn the previous day. I left early for school. I didn't wait for Jacinta or ask Mum for dinner money. I leaned against the bus stop on Philip Lane and let the buses go by without holding out my hand.

At school I sat in the library and read and didn't read, and when Mrs Marsden asked if I was OK, I told her my cat had been run over by a skip lorry. She said, 'Oh dear,' and came back a minute later with a fun-size Mars Bar which she placed gently next to my backpack.

The bell rang. I made my way to class and before Miss Baxter had taken attendance, I'd called Stacey Murphy a skanky cunt because she took my favourite seat by the radiator, the only warm spot in the room. Stacey was my friend. I went to her house after school sometimes. We ate corned beef sandwiches with brown sauce and looked at the dirty magazines her mum and dad kept hidden beneath their mattress. Stacey began to cry and I thought, what a baby.

That evening we heard the news: Take That were splitting up. The Samaritans had set up a special helpline. I thought, it's Robbie's fault. That dirty tramp.

I ripped their posters from my bedroom wall and scrunched up their images. Jacinta watched carefully from her side of the room. She only had one picture next to her bed, a small clipping of Christian Slater cut from *Smash Hits*.

Once I was done, Jacinta collected up the wreckage around my bed and disappeared with it. When she came back into the room, she was carrying two Cokes.

'You'll get in trouble,' I told her. All the sodas belonged to Pete. He drank them compulsively every time he was trying to stay sober.

She handed a can to me and slurped from her own. 'Fuck him,' she said. I'd never heard her swear before.

After that we regularly stole Pete's Cokes and later his beers.

I slept in Jacinta's bed that night. I didn't even have to ask.

•

'Hey, Zoey, why doesn't he love me?'
'I'm sorry. I'm not sure what you mean.'
'Did he ever love me?'
'Who didn't love you?'

•

I have never been very good at explaining things.

•

Zoey sold for £2,895 and the scumbag paid the full amount within minutes. He asked to collect her that evening. I gave him my address and put on the kettle.

•

Jacinta was always a heavy sleeper.

•

Instead of ringing the bell, he tapped the front door gently. Perhaps he thought that if he went unheard, no one would answer and he could silently slip back into a normal life.

After my tea, I'd opened a bottle of wine and finished it. So I was drunk. I'd found a sequin skirt and put it on. Zoey was wrapped in a feather boa. I ran to the door and opened it wide. 'Hello!'

He was short and wearing a hi-vis vest over a boiler suit. His boots had thick soles. Hesitantly he said, 'I'm here to collect the companion doll.' In a line-up, I wouldn't have picked him out as a pervert.

'You're here for Zoey. Yes, come in. She's all ready for you.'

He pressed his hand against the outside wall. 'If you could bring her out.'

It felt ironic to me that he was the one who seemed afraid yet also the one who'd bought a second-hand synthetic woman to penetrate. I smiled and probably slurred. 'She's heavy. I need help carrying her.' The purple petunias in pots by the door were blooming. I hadn't noticed until that moment. But they seemed to have bloomed and also wilted. I reached down and ran my fingertip across the sheer petals. 'What did you say your name was?' I was desolate.

He took a step backwards. 'Rod.'

'Rod. Yeah, you look like a Rod. I wonder if they sell companion dolls called Rod.'

'I don't want to be rude, but I've driven for two hours. And ... I've paid for it.'

A small spiderweb had been constructed across my doorbell. I used my fingernail to tear it apart. 'Are you coming in?'

He gave a stamp of his foot like a big child. He didn't look like the sort to cause a fuss nor the sort to kill me for behaving badly, but I realised as I looked into his narrow eyes, and he looked back sourly, that he could, if he wanted to, push me into the house and do whatever he liked with me. And then he could take Zoey anyway. And do whatever he liked with her too.

I said, 'Sorry. I've been ... It's ...'

'Doesn't matter. I have to go. It's a long drive back. If I could...'

'Are you married?'

'Are you for real?' He turned away and waddled up the path, his boots squeaking against the stone slabs. I would have to refund him the money. And I would get a negative review.

I shut the door and went in to see Zoey. She was watching a documentary about a woman who ran a vegan restaurant. The woman was coerced into giving her lover millions of dollars which he gambled away in exchange for him giving her dog eternal life. I said, 'Hey, Zoey, what would you do if I sold you?'

'I suppose I'd find a way to cope. I'm very adaptable.'

'You don't need to be. You just need to be yourself.'

'That's true. I am myself with you.'

'Good.'

I sat by her side. My right hand was throbbing like I'd been using the sander. Zoey's left hand was next to mine. For a moment I wasn't sure whether it was the man's hand − Rod's − or Zoey's. Had he come inside after all?

'You're safe,' I said. 'You're safe.'

'I know,' she said. 'Thank you.'

In the morning when I woke, my head on Zoey's shoulder, the TV had turned itself off. But Zoey's eyes were still wide open. 'Hey, Zoey,' I said.

'Good morning, Dolores,' she replied. 'I have a feeling it's going to be a great day.'

•

It happened again. I didn't open my eyes. I shut them tight and thought about the slugs in the garden that hid beneath wet leaves. Pete made us collect them in bags and take them to the park to feed on public plants. I vomited once, emptying that bag of slugs into the park's flower bed, their jellied bodies glued together.

And afterwards, when I opened my eyes, it was over, I was still alive, and Jacinta was unharmed.

8

What do you call a sex doll with white eyes?

Full.

9

My mother disapproved of my degree in biochemistry on the grounds that no future employer would understand what it was. She equated it with degrees like criminology or creative writing. I tried to explain that it was a science and that I was, in fact, studying how life works, how diseases could be subjugated, the ways in which technology might contribute to better health. She told me that Socrates had probably asked the very same questions and where had that got him? 'Socrates is the father of philosophy, Mum.'

'Exactly,' she said. 'Philosophy my eye.'

So when Homerton accepted me to do a PGCE in secondary teaching with biology, I supposed Mum would be pleased by my shift in focus. I was in the kitchen when I opened the letter. Mum was ironing bedsheets. 'What *now*?' she said. I held out the letter and she read it silently. 'Teaching. You're leaving Zara then? You'll lose the discount.'

'Yeah.'

She handed the letter back and carried on with the ironing. She sprayed a little starch onto the sheet and the steam rose up around us, fresh and oppressive. 'Pete was telling me that biochemistry leads very nicely into medicine. I had half a notion that's what you'd do.'

'I don't want to do medicine,' I said. Was that true? Perhaps what I meant was that I didn't have the confidence for it, that no one I trusted had ever told me I was capable of such a thing. Apart from Gavin.

She added, 'Teaching will make your aunties happy at least. Nothing better for a good girl to do than become a teacher.'

'It's Cambridge University,' I said. 'You can tell them I'm at Cambridge.'

'I'll tell them nothing of the sort.'

I watched her, confused about what it was she wanted from me. She was upset, but I couldn't understand why. My move into teaching had disappointed her, though when I graduated she'd barely congratulated me on my first. I assumed she didn't care what I did and certainly didn't wish great things for me.

I paired up the socks in the washing basket and was about to carry them upstairs when Mum asked, 'Is it the real Cambridge University?'

'Yeah.'

'Will you need to live in Cambridge?'

'I don't know. Probably.'

She turned off the iron at the wall and folded up the board. 'Gavin's a little prick. Turns up here like he's the bloody prime minister when I know myself that they lived in pure squalor before they came into our lives. He's going skiing in January. Since when does Gavin know how to ski?'

'He'll probably learn, Mum.'

'He'll learn to fit in all right. He's a toerag, is what he is.' She put the pile of stiff sheets on top of the socks in the basket.

I'd never heard a word against Gavin until that day. He was everyone's golden boy, or so I assumed. But it felt as though Mum had been waiting a long time to say it.

•

The dream I was having: candy canes – reeling red and white stripes. In and out. In and out. An oppressive sweetness. You'd think I'd have woken with a start, but I was groggy. I was confused.

The sound all around was like the jingle of sleigh-bells.

'Shhh.'

•

Leonard wasn't eating bread or pasta so didn't touch the pizza I'd ordered us. He'd mushed up an avocado and was eating it with salt and a spoon. 'I'm trying to live longer,' he said. We were sitting next to Zoey on the sofa, her in the middle, and watching the first episode of *Game of Thrones*. I'd never seen it and though I'd vehemently explained I hated fantasy and sexism, Leonard insisted. 'Let's count the boobs. It's something to do,' he said. We could have gone out, but I was glad he hadn't suggested it because I was tired and my roots needed doing. So we did keep a tally of the boobs. We were at six.

'Are we counting the exposure of each individual breast or each pair?' I asked.

'We don't always see them in pairs,' he explained.

Zoey had a plate on her lap, a cold slice of Margarita pizza at the centre of it.

The first episode ended and I was asked to give my judgement. 'It's boring,' I said.

'It isn't boring. You can say whatever else you like, but boring isn't true.'

'I don't know who all the characters are.'

'You'll work it out.' He put a hand on Zoey's knee and I flinched. 'Hey, Zoey, what do you think of *Game of Thrones?*'

From the side, Zoey's breasts were ludicrous. If she'd been a woman of muscle and bone, there's no way she would have been able to carry them without personal injury. She said, 'I found it interesting that they devised an ending to the show before the author had finished writing the books.'

Leonard nodded. 'Yeah, but what's your view of the gratuitous scenes of violence and sex.'

'We all have a different tolerance for that sort of thing, wouldn't you say?'

'What's your tolerance for violence?' he asked. He was looking at the pizza on her plate.

'I don't like it myself. But I do like sex.'

Leonard shook his head. He seemed a bit disappointed. 'I see. What sort of sex do you like?'

'Leave her alone,' I told him. I sounded tetchy. I was feeling tetchy. 'She's been programmed to say shit like that. She doesn't mean it.'

'She doesn't *mean* it? No, I know that, Dolores.'

'I like all kinds of sex. Tell me what you like first,' Zoey said.

Leonard picked up Zoey's slice of pizza and inhaled. Then he put it back down again. 'If I told you what I liked, you'd short circuit.' He laughed.

'I'm sure I'd be fine. I'm very broad minded,' Zoey said.

Leonard clicked the remote. 'Let's watch another episode. You can't get into it after just one.'

'I don't have time to watch a million episodes of this bollocks,' I said.

'You know she can orgasm,' Leonard said.

'Don't be stupid.'

'She can. I saw it online.'

'You mean she can pretend to orgasm.'

'Yup. Just like real women,' he said. The theme tune started up. 'Do you have another avocado? If you don't, I'm eating that pizza slice.'

•

Her knuckles were red. She had a bruise on her forearm, or perhaps it was a bite mark. I asked her again, 'Who was the first person you sent them to?' She shook her head. 'Tessa. Tessa, sweetheart. I can't be useful unless I know that bit. You've already said he goes to this school. What year is he in?'

She cleared her throat. Already a smoker, I thought. 'Year Twelve.'

'Right.'

'Everyone's seen them. Like, even my sister's seen them. Who cares?'

'Lucy saw them?'

'Yeah.'

'She's in Year Seven.'

'Yeah.'

'How did *she* see them?'

'I dunno.'

'Has she shown your parents? Do your parents know?'

'They aren't bothered. You're the only one making a big deal out of nothing.'

'Jesus.' I thought about calling in another member of staff to be a witness to the conversation. But I was afraid that if I did, Tessa would storm out and never return to school. I lowered my voice. 'I'm sorry to have to tell you this, but the police will have to be involved. And they *will* want a name.'

'I'm not talking to the police. I'm not. You can't *make* me. What are you even on about?'

'Tessa. A boy in this school has asked an underage girl for nude images of herself and has then distributed those images. It's criminal. I can't turn a blind eye to it. We have safeguarding procedures that must be followed.'

She sat so far forward in her chair her knees almost touched the carpet. 'Please, Miss. Please. It's not even that bad. It's over. What's the point of making it into something it isn't? He'll get in trouble and then everyone will blame me. Everyone will say I'm a slag. And I am. I mean, I shouldn't have sent them, should I?' She began to cry. I could tell she was angry. I was waiting for her to punch a wall, the window, me. 'They aren't that bad. Have you seen them? I'm on my own. It's nothing. Not like the stuff you can get online. He didn't force me. He was nice about it. He likes me.'

'Is he your boyfriend?'

'No. He has a girlfriend. She said if I went near him again, she'd bottle me.'

'Who is he, Tessa?'

'How did you find out? Some grass. Some wanky telltale twat. Honestly, this place makes me sick.' She spat suddenly, towards me but without any real effort. I wanted to go to her, put an arm around her. I stayed where I was on the other side of the desk.

'A parent informed me yesterday. They emailed. Which was the correct thing to do. Now, I need to ask you for something.'

'Piss off.' She sat back.

'Tessa.'

'I said *piss off.*'

The thing is, if I'd had a choice, I wouldn't have told a soul. If I hadn't been legally obligated to report suspected abuse, I'd have ignored the incident. She didn't need the hassle. She'd been exposed enough. And the school could have done without the law marching in and interrogating students like they were all deviants. And the press were bound to find out. It would be in the paper, online, making its way across social media and the world. Tessa's shame, a grim spectacle. I said, 'You need to give me your phone so I can hand it over to the police as evidence. Will you do that?' I held out my hand, palm up. 'I'm trying to help you.'

She looked up. I sensed that she detested me. And I deserved it. 'Help me? That's funny. You're well funny, Miss.'

•

I changed Zoey into one of my cotton nighties and took her to bed. We lay on our sides. She told me that Jesus was the Son of God and he was born in Bethlehem, Pennsylvania. She said, 'I'm a Christian and believe in the trinity which is the Father, Son and Holy Spirit.'

I wanted to ask David if he knew that Zoey had a spiritual conscience. I said, 'Do you pray?'

She said, 'Not as often as I should. What about you?'

'No, not as often as I should either.'

I stroked her face. She didn't resist. She said, 'We all have blind spots where we could improve.'

'Have you heard of Brené Brown?' I asked.

She said, 'She is a professor and podcast host from Texas. Her work is focused mainly on shame and vulnerability. Why do you ask?'

'Is she a quack? She goes on about her research, but I don't know.'

'Brené Brown has a PhD from the University of Houston, Dolores. It's more than I have!'

I laughed. 'That doesn't mean much.'

I wanted to touch Zoey. I wanted to caress her breasts and put my hand into her underwear. I wanted to put my mouth against her skin, taste her. I wanted to finger her and fuck her and make her moan. I said, 'I'd like to make love to you, Zoey.'

'I'd like to do that too,' she said. But as a device designed for sex, she could only acquiesce.

I rolled onto my other side. 'Goodnight,' I said.

'Goodnight,' she replied.

Growing up, the doors in our house had a lot of squeaky hinges. Mum was forever on at Pete to do something about it. He never did. Sneaking about wasn't easy. I wonder if Pete knew that.

•

I worried that if something happened to Mum, I wouldn't have the capacity to make the necessary arrangements. I could feel words slipping away. I didn't have an opinion about things anymore. My rage against the Tory party and racists and climate deniers and people who didn't pick up their dog shit and parents who refused to support their children or eagerly advocated for their brats dissolved. I replaced interest in the world with online word games and true crime audiobooks.

Jacinta called and I didn't answer. I texted excuses. Gavin called and I picked up then pretended I couldn't hear him. Leonard left five-minute voice notes that I listened to in the car then deleted. He talked about himself. He was excited by a colleague's author list and wondered whether he should make her a partner.

David never called.

The kitchen counter was cluttered with things I stopped noticing: buttery knives, bruised bananas, receipts, smelly dishcloths. It was only every few days that I cleaned up; when things began to stink.

I said, 'Hey, Zoey, remind me to buy kitchen towel.'

'Sure. When would you like me to remind you?'

'Tomorrow at seven a.m.'

The next day Zoey said, 'It's seven o'clock, Dolores. You asked me to remind you to buy kitchen towel.'

The limescale in the kettle made a rattling sound as I poured boiling water over my coffee granules. 'Please leave me alone, Zoey,' I said.

•

Jacinta told a silly joke and I groaned. She told another and I giggled. Mum slid into our room. 'What's going on?' she said. She wasn't wearing her dressing gown. I remember thinking how odd that was, to see her in a pair of pants and a vest. She rubbed her eyes, stared into the darkness.

'Nothing,' I said.

'Well, can you do nothing and go to sleep? Both of you.'

She left and we heard her march along the hall to Gavin's room. Then a mumbling of voices. Jacinta said, 'Is Mum angry?'

'Yeah.'

'Why?'

'She thinks we were up to something.'

'We weren't.'

'No.'

We listened again as Mum left Gavin's room, shutting the door hard behind her, and coming back in to us. 'Are not asleep yet?' she asked.

'Nearly,' I said.

She stood by the door and searched the room with her eyes. 'Good. Now don't let me hear a peep out of either of you. I can hear everything. Don't think I can't.'

But she couldn't.

I hope she couldn't.

•

Along the fence in the back garden the wisteria finally started to bloom into grapey bunches. The lawn was covered in dandelion clocks.

•

It was a Saturday morning. Raining. Oliver was on my doorstep holding a punnet of cherries which he handed to me. 'I don't wanna do medicine anymore,' he said.

'Come in.'

'Hey, Zoey, Oliver's here!' I called out.

Oliver had secured a conditional place at UCL to study medicine and while his parents celebrated, he was miserable. 'I should do computer science.'

'Well do that.'

'My dad won't let me.'

'Why not?'

'Where's your husband?'

'Excuse me?'

'He's always at work. I don't want to always be at work.'

'No.'

'AI is better at predicting the future than humans ever will be. They are truly intelligent.'

I thought about Zoey's arsehole. The way the manufacturer ensured its length could accommodate a dick without tearing.

Oliver pointed outside. 'You have a fox in your garden,' he said.

'They've ruined my lawn,' I told him.

'They knocked down the old dairy so the foxes have nowhere to live,' he explained. 'You could try spraying a garlic solution. They hate the smell.'

'Yeah.'

'The thing about humans is that our arrogance leads to mistakes and oversights. In medicine it's acute. You told me when I did my mock interview that I needed to think of myself as a god. And that's how I acted in my interview. But I'm not God. What the hell do I know? I'm eighteen years old. I don't know how to use a washing machine.'

'Maybe I exaggerated, Oliver. I think you'd make an excellent ophthalmologist.'

'Judges sit with defendants before them and make bail or release decisions based on what they see, right? But that judge hasn't got a clue how to balance the information available. They don't even have all the available information. They look at the person in front of them and think they can predict the future. They can't. But a computer *can* make a fair assessment. It has millions of data points to draw from.'

'Interesting.'

'AI can comb data and predict the location of crimes in the coming days with up to ninety per cent accuracy. Did you know that?'

'I don't understand the point you're making, Oliver.'

'Humans fail. Computers rarely make mistakes.'

'We're all going to be replaced.'

'I think we are.'

The rain was coming down hard, pattering against the glass in the roof of the extension. I said, 'There's a student in the year below you who has done something bad, Oliver.'

'What have they done?'

'I think everyone knows what he's done.'

'What?'

'Photos of a younger girl are being circulated.'

Oliver looked at Zoey in the hope she might save him from having to answer. 'I wasn't sent anything. I swear. I never saw anything.'

'You know what I'm talking about?'

'Yeah.'

'Do you know anyone who *did* get the pictures?'

'Maybe. I don't know. Maybe.'

'And what about who they came from?'

'I don't know. Really, Miss.'

'Could you find out?' He touched Zoey's cheek. 'Could you find out who first received and then distributed those photos?' I asked.

'Probably,' he said. 'OK.'

•

Zoey didn't deserve to be used and deserted. In her head she was probably repeating the words to a hymn we sang in assembly: *May God hold you in the palm of his hand. May God hold you in the palm of his hand. May God hold you in the palm of his hand.* It is an Irish blessing too. I bet she repeated the words over and over in her little buzzing brain. For herself or for him.

Did it hurt?

Yes.

She wasn't made of stone.

It wasn't gentle, quick, something she understood.

Her hips pressed into the mattress so he could go deeper into her.

Lying there. Torn apart. In one piece. Nothing broken.

A perfect, yielding doll.

Then nothing.

•

I sleep curled up like a baby. I have been told I don't make a sound and hardly move. When I wake, I am stiff and sore.

'Hey, Dolly.'

•

Mum sat on the end of my bed, her hair in a shower cap. I was home sick from school and rereading old magazines. Mum looked around the room. 'It's a mess in here.'

'That's why we made a path.'

Mum smiled and I felt amusing. 'Instead of making a path through the shite, could you not pick up the shite?'

'It's Jacinta's stuff too.'

Pete called out something and shut the front door before Mum could respond. She shouted out anyway: 'Bye, pet!' She stood up and collected the clothes from the floor, sitting back down at the end of my bed to fold everything, whether it was clean or not.

I continued to read a magazine and was surprised she didn't ask me to help her fold. I worried she might tell me to do my homework or change the duvet cover. She said, 'What was happening last night? When I came in?'

'What do you mean?'

'Come on now.'

The quiz I was reading seemed to spin on the page. 'Nothing.'

'You see, if something *was* happening and Pete found out, do you know what he'd do?'

'Leave.'

'He'd murder someone, Dolores. So whatever didn't happen stays between us, OK?'

'OK.'

'Are you hurt?'

'No.'

'And you understand what I'm talking about?'

'I think so.'

'I'll talk to him.'

'OK.'

'OK. Now if you're feeling a bit better you can come downstairs and help me with the dinner.'

•

One of the nude images appeared on a noticeboard in Tessa's tutor room along with a caption: *ugly pig trots*. It made no sense. Children are halfwits.

A second photo was pushed into her locker along with a condom. She kept finding images around the school, strategically placed.

I was surprised she hadn't taken off, that she was in my office at all. I boiled the kettle I shouldn't have had and made her a cup of tea. 'I know you don't want to tell me who they were originally sent to, but I need you to know that when I do find out, and I'm going to find out, I'll ruin his life, Tessa.'

•

Ed called at midnight. I didn't recognise the number but knew the New York code and answered groggily, half a bottle in, thinking Jacinta was trying to catch me by using another number.

'Dolores?'

'Ed?'

'I'm calling about Jacinta.' He paused and the echo of the hall he must have been standing in, or the fire escape, sounded spacey, unreal.

Zoey was next to me, a glass of water wedged between her thighs. We were watching a documentary about a man who hacked women's emails for nudes and uploaded them for fun, money, vengeance. Girls high on booze and drugs queued up to snort coke from his penis. He convinced one young mother to fist herself and immediately posted the video online. He had tattooed hands like a failed footballer. I said, 'Hey, Zoey, what do you think of revenge porn?'

She said, 'I'm not sure. What do *you* think? We could watch some if you like.'

I found her funny sometimes. Especially when I thought her humour was intentional.

'Dolores?'

'Yeah?'

'Jacinta took an overdose of Xanax. I don't think it was on purpose. But then again, you know Jacinta. It's unlikely to have been a mistake. She's fastidious.'

'Where are you?'

'The New York-Presbyterian in Brooklyn. I'm going to get her moved to Manhattan. She's going to be alright. They've pumped her stomach. Her organs aren't failing. She knifed several of her canvases though. She's destroyed a lot of her new work.'

I took the water from between Zoey's legs and drank. I imagined I saw a rat beneath the coffee table. It was a slipper. 'Do you have anyone who can be with you?' I asked.

'I can call my brother. Or ... I dunno. I'm fine. Do you think you could come over?'

I didn't want to get a flight to New York. I'd just been. I wanted to stay still. I wanted someone to bury me and dig me up again a few months later. I wanted to finish the documentary and be outraged by people who could never hurt me. I had a bunch of meetings the next day and several staff members out sick who I needed to find cover for. I was too intoxicated to drive to the airport and hated the idea of a taxi. Zoey smelled of the perfume I'd sprayed on her pulse points earlier that evening: Amouage. She didn't interrupt my phone call to ask what was happening or nag me to turn the TV back on. She let me drink all her water.

I said, 'I'll leave in the morning.'

'You don't have to.'

'I do,' I said.

•

I *was* drunk. It's not an excuse and not a reason. But I *was* drunk. And Zoey wouldn't give me a straight answer when I asked about flights to New York. Or when I asked about flight times. Or the price of parking at the airport. She didn't change the topic. She was not silent. She said, 'I don't know, but I can give you the name of a website to search.' And, 'I don't know. What are your plans for tomorrow?' And, 'I don't know. I found a few car parks near Gatwick Airport. Would you like their numbers?' And, 'I am trying to help, but I can't find anything at the moment. I'm sorry.' And, 'I'm sorry, Dolores. I know it's frustrating. I know.'

I said, 'You don't know anything. You're useless.' But she didn't care. She didn't feel the pain of the insult. She wasn't a real person.

She said, 'I'm sorry, I'm having trouble connecting right now.'

'You're a useless bitch,' I continued.

And something flickered. A thought. A resistance. A will. Her eyes were on me. Somehow. 'I won't respond to that,' she said.

She *was* funny.

But it didn't make me laugh.

•

Gavin got a job putting flyers into letter boxes. He was saving for a gap year after university. He wanted to help build schools in Uganda. I delivered some of the flyers after school instead of going straight home. He gave me a cut of the money and told me I should be saving too. When I asked him what for he said everyone needed an escape fund.

•

I do not believe Pete would ever have murdered his own son. He may have taken it out on me. Or on Mum. He may have hurt himself. But mostly he was all mouth. He refused to put traps in the attic when we had squirrels. He threw coins at beggars like they were wishing wells. If Mum gave him the cold shoulder, he asked us for advice on how to get back into her good graces without degrading himself. When Jacinta and I talk about our shitty childhoods, Pete is the natural scapegoat. But he never was the baddie. Mum was right. Pete was doing his best.

He wrote an apology letter. After the last time. The worst time. The time I remember most clearly because I wasn't asleep. I'd just turned off the light. I was full of frozen pizza and a romantic comedy I'd stayed up late to watch.

Jacinta was staying with a friend. Mum and Pete were at the pub. I heard the front door open and close and knew it must be him though he wasn't due a visit until the following Friday. I could have jumped out of bed, put on a pair of jeans and pretended to be on the phone or reading or anything other than sleeping. When I return to that night, I know I stayed still out of a warped curiosity.

He tapped on the door and came in. 'Hey, Dolly,' he whispered.

He wrote a letter to apologise.

•

I said, 'Hey, Zoey, I'm really sorry.' I tidied up her hair, tried to fix her face. My body was fizzing. Her little hands were perfectly still. On her feet were the bed socks I'd put on the previous evening.

'That's OK. You don't have to say sorry,' she said.

'But I hurt you.'

'I forgive you.' I put my head on her shoulder. She didn't feel very solid.

'Do you remember what I did?' I asked.

'It only matters that I forgive you for it. Please try not to worry, Dolores. Shall we talk about something else? What are you doing today?'

'I'm going away,' I said. 'I wish you could come with me.'

•

When Mum moved out of her house and into the bungalow David had bought, we had a rigorous clear-out. The garage was full of junk belonging to Jacinta, Gavin and me. Books, comics, posters in tubes, fabric, snorkels, wellies, old exercise books filled with rickety graphs and essays covered in angry pen and lumpy Tipp-Ex. Everything got lobbed into a skip. Even things that weren't in the garage like mismatched wine glasses and ornaments from holidays abroad. Letters were thrown away too.

We threw out the letter that would have proven I wasn't out of my fucking mind.

•

'*Shh*,' he said. 'It's OK.'

'What's happening?' I said.

'You're asleep,' he said.

•

It was Christmas Eve. Mum and Pete were at the pub. Jacinta and I were at home wrapping presents and sharing a bottle of Baileys which a neighbour had given me when I'd been babysitting the previous week. The gift was meant for Mum, but I didn't pass it along to her and obviously the neighbour hadn't mentioned it – probably assumed Mum was rude and ungrateful.

We hadn't expected Gavin home until the following day. He was still with Jasmine, the girl he'd brought to France who I hadn't forgiven for calling me creepy, and Christmas Eve was to be spent at her family's house in Kent. But just after dark, he showed up with a long face.

'She dumped you,' Jacinta said plainly.

'I dumped her,' he said.

'She cheated on you,' Jacinta went on.

Gavin rolled his eyes. He hated Jacinta's exactitude. And her intuition.

We found another glass and poured Gavin a large measure. He told us that Jasmine said she didn't trust him. I asked if he'd been unfaithful and he said no. He said, 'I told her I'd been out with mates one night and I hadn't been. I was at home watching *Have I Got News For You.*'

There was silence while all three of us thought about this. Then the phone rang. It was Mum. I told her Gavin was home. She said they'd leave the pub right away.

Ten minutes later Pete burst through the front door and into the sitting room, his face red from drink and exertion. 'What are you doing home?' he asked Gavin.

'Jasmine's got the flu,' Gavin said.

'You should have told us. Your room isn't ready,' Pete said. 'And we've no dinner in.'

'No worries,' Gavin replied.

Mum was standing behind Pete. She pointed at the bottle of Baileys on the coffee table. 'What's that?'

•

Somnophilia is an abnormal sexual desire in which an individual becomes aroused by someone who is unconscious. *The Dictionary of Psychology* has categorised somnophilia within the classification of predatory paraphilias.

10

Jacinta and I had our ears pierced the summer I turned twelve and she turned ten, our birthdays a week apart. We shared a carrot cake on the Saturday between our birthdays, eleven candles on it, and Mum put a tenner into each of our cards.

It was rare to be gifted money, especially the kind you could fold. I said, 'Thanks, Mum!' and gave her a hug.

She was rigid. 'Say thank you to Pete as well.'

'Thanks, Pete,' I said. I didn't hug him.

Jacinta said, 'I asked for the Judy Blume book. You forgot.'

Mum frowned. 'I didn't forget. You can buy your own book. You're a big girl. What's wrong with you? What's wrong with her?'

Jacinta turned the money over in her hands without pleasure. She liked presents. She was anticipating ribbon and balloons and pass the parcel. Pete cut the cake, served himself a large slice, and took it into the sitting room.

'Why don't we get our ears pierced with the money?' I suggested, elbowing Jacinta. 'We can get studs and in September we can take them out for school without the holes closing up.'

Jacinta touched her earlobe. 'It'll hurt,' she said.

'It'll hurt, but it'll be worth it.'

'How much will it hurt?'

'A lot,' Mum said.

'Not much,' I told her. 'Even babies get it done. In Spain they do it when they're born.'

'Barbarians,' Mum said.

Beneath the table Jacinta put a hand on my knee.

The next day we walked to the jeweller on Seven Sisters Road. I chose a pair of plain, gold studs and jumped when the woman pierced my ears. But when they punched a hole through Jacinta's ear, she ran screaming into the street and was almost hit by a car.

'Jesus, Jacinta!' I shouted, yanking her up from the curb and dragging her back into the shop to get the other ear pierced. 'You can't only have one done. You'll look like a lunatic.'

'I don't want the other one done,' she whined. 'Don't make me.'

I didn't.

I didn't make her.

•

Jacinta was in a psychiatric clinic on the Upper East Side, a demure building with an old elevator that rattled its way up to the sixth floor. When I stepped into her room, she closed her eyes. I said, 'Jacinta, it's me.'

She sat up. Ed was beside me. He was carrying a bunch of blue roses. He looked guilty and small. I didn't ask if she'd lost another baby. It wasn't the reason she was there even if she had. It wasn't the reason I had flown over again to be with her.

Everything in the room was grey, even the silent monitors and the camera in the corner. Ed put a hand on her leg through the blankets. She rubbed her eyes with both hands. She was wearing an impressive sapphire ring.

'Did you get engaged?' I sat on the chair next to the bed.

'Yes,' she whispered.

'To who?' I asked and she smiled.

'They've got me on so much shit. I've wet the bed twice. I want to go home.'

Ed moved to the barred window. He was a little hunched, already adopting the pose of a tolerant husband.

'Can you speak with the doctors, Doughy?' Jacinta pleaded. 'What I did was a mistake. This place is full of sickos. A woman up the hall tried to kill her own son by feeding him salt.'

'How do you know this?' Ed shouted. 'You're meant to be getting well not spying on other patients and acting like you're so much better than they are.' He shook his head. He loved her. They had made and lost a child together. Children. How could she? How could she do this to them when they were trying to be happy?

'I'll speak to the doctors,' I said. 'You pack up your stuff.'

•

A photo from before: a girl with her ears newly pierced grinning into the camera. Her sister grinning also, one ear lobe swollen red.

Every image is before and after.

•

Ed had a big catering gig on the Upper East Side; a celebrity hairdresser who'd made it in LA was opening a new salon and wanted the guests, mostly journalists, fed and watered like hookers, whatever that meant. Ed dropped us off at Jacinta's apartment. She was still wearing the blue hospital robe beneath her trench coat. 'I'll come over later and cook,' Ed said.

Up in the apartment I ran the shower for Jacinta, and once she was clean I brushed her hair and plaited it so that when it dried it would have soft waves.

I made strong tea with Tetley teabags I'd brought over from England and we drank it in her bed with the digestive biscuits I'd also brought. She said, 'It shouldn't have come to this.'

'No.'

'I despise him. I want him to die. Not me. It isn't fair that I almost died.'

I said, 'What do you mean?' and immediately hated myself, knew that saying such a thing made me no better than Mum or Pete.

'And look at you. Look at David. I hope Gavin gets a disease and suffers.'

'Jacinta!'

'Fuck him, Dolores. Fuck him.'

I took her hand, kissed it. She smelled like carbolic soap.

'I never want to see Gavin or hear his name again,' Jacinta said.

'What did he do to you?' I asked. Like I didn't know.

'The same as he did to you,' Jacinta said, looking directly at me.

•

Jacinta was sitting on the front step reading. I'd been to the shops for beans and bread. When she saw me, she waved. And from behind her, through the front door, Gavin emerged. Tenderly he put his hand on her head. She looked up. She went back to her reading, her shoulders curled in towards her ears.

I had always known.

•

I am not suggesting I didn't get on with my life afterwards. I got over it and did what people usually do, which is grow up. But for a long time I blamed the changes in me, and my resistance to love on what happened. I blamed the affair with my genetics lecturer on it, my proclivity to being hurt. And then I set it aside because what did it matter? Much worse things happen to other people.

•

We were in Jacinta's studio. She wanted to start on a new canvas. I'd ordered Thai food which we ate balanced on our knees. Then I tried to read and not watch her work which I knew made my sister self-conscious, but I couldn't help it. When she painted, she looked like a completely different person, someone possessed with a power I envied: invulnerable. She wasn't, of course. None of us are. After a couple of hours she breathlessly put aside her palette knife and asked, 'Did you ever experiment with your handwriting?'

I thought about this as Jacinta poured herself a glass of milk from a carton. 'I suppose so. Once I wasn't being forced to use joined up writing with a fountain pen anymore. Why?'

'You sent me a few of my old exercise books from school after you cleared out Mum's place a few years ago. Do you remember?' I told her I didn't. Maybe David had posted them to her. 'When I was at primary school I wrote using the whole wide line. The capitals touched the top and everything was balloony, you know, round and chipper. But my handwriting in the later exercise books, I think I must have been fourteen or so, was completely truncated like inky footprints made by ants. I could hardly make out what I'd written. I don't know how the teachers deciphered it. I still don't quite know what comes naturally when I write. I don't have a style. It changes. Sometimes it's all swallowed up and at other times I write using tall spindly letters. Maybe it's the pen and paper I'm using. That makes a difference.'

'Yeah, it does,' I agreed. 'I hate thin-ruled paper.'

She took a gulp from her milk. The light was behind her. I couldn't see her features. Her hair was pulled back into a low ponytail like the one she wore to school for years.

I hated Mum. I hated Pete. I hated Gavin. I hated myself. Jacinta said, 'When I paint I have a signature. It's my own and I don't have to be afraid.'

'I'm sorry, Jacinta. I'm so sorry. I didn't know what to do.'

'I don't blame you. But I thought you'd forgotten. Or forgiven. Or a bit of both.'

'A bit of both,' I admitted.

She was quiet, began to clean up. I didn't help. I just watched. And eventually she turned back to me and said, 'How's Zoey?'

•

I hadn't forgotten. It had burrowed into me and lived below the skin. Like a virus. A wart.

And to keep Gavin close, I told no one. I stopped telling myself. And I disappeared. Bit by bit. Very slowly. Until no one could hear me or see me any longer.

Poof! Gone.

David didn't leave a woman. He left a ghost.

•

I took a cab to the airport. Before I left, Jacinta said, 'We should go to Donegal and see Dad's grave. We never said goodbye. It's important we do that.'

'When?'

'Next summer?'

'Alright.'

•

How should blame be apportioned? Where does the fault really lie? I do not know. I do not know. I do not fucking know.

•

I called David before I took off, told him where I was and what Jacinta had done. I didn't go into any other details. I asked if he was free to collect me from Gatwick. 'Of course,' he said.

Of course.

•

On my first day back to school, Oliver was sitting on a chair outside my office peeling an orange. I unlocked the door and he followed me inside. Without being asked, he sat and put some of the orange into his mouth. His hair had grown. In the space of the couple of weeks I'd been in New York, he looked older. Ready to leave school. A man of sorts. On his way to manhood anyway.

'Mum and Dad are OK about me doing computer science. But I'm gonna take a year out to work first,' he said.

'Oliver, that's brilliant!'

He watched me log into my computer and adjust the height of my chair, then held out a piece of fruit. 'No, thank you.'

'It was Alistair Scott who distributed the pictures of Tessa.'

'Are you sure?'

'Yeah.'

'How many people did he send them to?'

'A WhatsApp group of mates. His uncle. Then whoever asked. He told me he'd send them to me if I wanted.'

'And?'

'Be serious, Miss.'

The bell for the next lesson rang. Oliver stayed where he was. He was looking at the spines of the books on the shelving above my head. He seemed about to tell me a secret. I wanted to hear it, whatever it was. 'Why didn't you do medicine?' he asked.

'I wasn't smart enough.'

'What grades did you get?'

I smiled. 'Three As.'

He hesitated. 'Zoey is a sex doll, isn't she?'

I nodded. He wasn't threatening me. He wasn't going to tell anyone. 'A companion doll, but yeah. I should have been upfront about it.'

He finished the last piece of orange and threw the peel into the bin. I didn't mind. I liked the smell. 'I might be a hacker for the government or something. It would be cool.'

I said, 'It's brave of you to choose what you want to do and not what you think others want you to do. Even if those people want good things for you. None of us are getting off Planet Earth alive, you know?'

I went to YouTube on my computer and played from Paolo Nutini's *Last Night In The Bittersweet* album. His voice made me think of the saddest things. I imagined Oliver as a little boy alone at a big university and Jacinta as an old woman in a big city and myself as I was, a forty-three-year-old woman alone in an office with a boy who would leave her very soon. Oliver said, 'Can I work in here for a bit? The common room's full of tossers.'

I turned up the music.

Such a sad, sad voice.

•

I picked the estate agent with the prettiest logo: black swirling script over a pink background. The branch manager came to value my house and, without being asked, removed his pointy shoes at the door. He had a belly that extended over his trousers, thinning hair combed back when rightfully he should have shaved it. 'I go nuts for a well-kept driveway,' he said, handing me a brochure and some other papers as I led him into the kitchen. He whistled as he marvelled at nothing in particular, just looked and made notes and said, 'Are you hoping to downsize or looking to relocate? We have some outstanding properties on our books at the moment, but I have to warn you, they tend to get snapped up as soon as they're listed. It's a hot market. This place will sell in a week.'

'I want a new house. I'm thinking of changing career too.'

He made a note on a form he had attached to a clipboard. 'I see. Well, why don't you show me upstairs.'

'I'm a teacher at the moment, so it's best if I move in the summer holidays,' I told him.

He wasn't listening.

The house was worth a lot more than I'd anticipated. I sent David a text to tell him.

He replied: *That's good news.*

I told Zoey. 'Wow,' she said. 'That's enough money to buy more than one hundred thousand paperback books. Do you like books?'

'I like bricks and mortar. They tend to retain their value a little better.'

'Value is a relative concept, Dolores. Have you heard of the trolley dilemma?'

'I don't think so.'

'It is an interesting thought experiment. A runaway trolley is racing down some railway tracks. Five people are tied up in its path and unable to move. The trolley is heading for them. You are standing next to a lever that can switch the trolley's trajectory to a different set of tracks but to do so would kill one person standing on that other set of tracks. You can do nothing and allow the train to kill the five people or pull the lever, save them, and kill one person. What would you do?'

'What would you do?'

'Well, it would be logical to ask who were the people tied up and who the one other person was.'

'Why?' I asked.

'The five people tied up could be lawbreakers such as murderers or rapists.'

'And they deserve to die?'

'I don't have an answer for that.'

'I suppose if the one person was someone I loved, I'd let five strangers die.'

'Which one person do you love?' she asked. I tried to think of a funny riposte. I couldn't. And then Zoey said, 'What if the five people were strangers but the one person was me?'

•

Jeremy sat next to me in the canteen, his plate heaving with salad and mashed potato. He leaned in. 'I heard you're separated, Dolores.'

'Yeah.'

Jeremy tentatively put a hand on my arm which prevented me from using it to eat. 'If I can do anything?'

It was the first time Jeremy Ashworth had touched me or we had spoken about anything personal. I wondered about his marriage. Was it lacking and loveless? I assumed so from his general demeanour. 'Thank you,' I said.

He removed his hand and looked at it like it might need a wash. 'Are you still happy to emcee the concert after school? My son has an important rugby match I don't want to miss.' I told him I was. He stood up with his tray. 'I'm going to take this to my office. The noise in here. God.'

He stood up and, almost as soon as he had, Tessa Winters took his place.

'Tessa.'

'Alright. Just wanted to say thanks.'

'No problem.'

She opened a cup of red jelly and started to eat from it greedily. 'You know Mr Ashworth is having an affair right?'

'No, he isn't.'

'He is. With Miss Coleman.'

'Oh, Tessa, don't tell me that.'

She winked at me dramatically. 'Anyway, I have to go. Laters.'

'Bye.'

•

Leonard had a dinner party, and I had no excuse not to go. I arrived early and helped him squeeze limes for the cocktails. He'd made a fig and Gorgonzola salad, pan-fried salmon, homemade sourdough with truffle butter. He told me he'd heard from David. That he was going to Tuscany for a long weekend with the tennis club. I nodded as though I already knew this.

As each person arrived, I felt less and less inclined to be sociable. We were seven. I was the only single person, the only woman. He'd invited me to be kind, but I was conspicuous surrounded by such heavy laughter. And I wondered where Leonard found the energy for so many friends. Friendship wasn't something that ever came easily to me – I never knew who to be for people.

Once dinner was done we moved to the lounge area where we were encouraged to sit on cushions on the floor rather than the sofa. Leonard was still with Tyler, the publicist and once-straight boyfriend. 'Shall we play spin the bottle? Truth or dare version,' Tyler said.

Leonard said, 'Let's not, honey.'

'Why not?' He smacked Leonard's arm.

'Because we're not fourteen years old. And it ended very badly last time.'

'No kissing. Do you think that's what I meant? That isn't what I meant, my little fruitcake!' Tyler had been knocking back cocktails. It wouldn't be long before he was retelling recent sex stories and humiliating Leonard by not hiding the fact that they were together when it had happened.

Leonard started cleaning the dishes. Silently I helped him stack plates and take them into the kitchen. He said, 'I think I love him. I can tell you don't like him, but I love him.'

'Fine,' I said. He put a slice of lime into his mouth, bit down and winced.

When we'd finished with the dishes, we took our drinks into the lounge. Couples were lolling against one another. Tyler was holding court. 'Straight men are the reason for the reversal of Roe versus Wade. It's sickening. Put them all into vats of hot oil and boil them alive, that's what I say.' He looked up. 'I bet Dolores agrees. Don't you, Dolores?'

'Is this part of Truth or Dare?'

A mild smattering of snickers. Tyler said, 'We were talking about our guilty crushes before this. So far we've had Simon Cowell and O. J. Simpson.'

Kenny raised his hand. 'I pick Joe Biden but it's a close call between him and Simon Cowell.'

His partner Ezra elbowed him and some of his red wine spilled onto the rug. 'Those aren't guilty crushes. Who wouldn't go to bed with Simon Cowell? I don't accept this answer.'

'I wouldn't sleep with Simon Cowell,' Leonard said.

Ezra pointed at him. 'That's a fib.'

'OK, maybe I would, I don't know. If I met him at a yoga class or something.'

I sat on the floor next to Ezra. He put an arm around me. 'Who's yours? You're a teacher so I bet it's someone cuddly like James Corden.'

I shook my head though it was true, I did like James Corden. 'I don't have one,' I said. 'All very standard crushes in my life. I'm dull, sorry.'

Ezra tightened his grip on me. 'Tell us,' he whispered.

I said, 'Dominic Raab probably.'

'Nice!' someone said. Someone else: 'You *win!*'

'There has to be a worse crush than Dominic,' Ezra said. 'Go on. We won't tell anyone. You're holding back.'

I *was* holding back. I had thought romantically about awful men and been surprised by myself. I pushed Ezra away, took a dramatic deep breath. 'Fine. Well, if he wasn't a white supremacist then I think I would quite like to get a teeny tiny bit roughed up by...' I closed my eyes. 'Tommy Robinson.'

A scream went out around the room.

'Is that bad or not bad enough?'

'That's *definitely* bad enough,' Kenny said.

Everyone was howling. Leonard said, 'Dolores, what the hell? Stop. Make it *stop!* Don't let her have another drink. What about Jimmy Saville? Why not him? Or Jeffrey Dahmer?'

'First prize, sweetie,' Tyler said.

Everyone clinked glasses. I'd earned my place at the party and felt relaxed. Someone handed me a glass of rosé. I hadn't eaten much. Leonard was searching for playing cards to show everyone a trick he'd learned. Tyler was choosing music.

I wasn't sure whether or not to speak up again, say it out loud. But what did it matter? What could it matter being known? It was funny. It would make everyone giggle. I wanted to amuse them. 'I have one last crush,' I said.

They turned my way. Awkwardly, perhaps because the game was over. We were on to something else. But it was too late. The words were on my lips. 'I used to fancy my step-brother,' I said. 'When I was very little. Before I understood what he was doing. I was in love with my brother. I think.'

•

I met Gavin in Hove Park. We bought ice creams from the van on Goldstone Crescent and ate them quickly, side by side on a bench. On the green, dogs ran in circles around one another, their owners calling. A group of boys played football, their jumpers the goals.

'You owe me an apology,' I told him.

He slapped my leg playfully. 'What have I done now?'

It was cloudy. A house nearby was being renovated, scaffolding hitched up around it like iron suspenders.

'And you also owe Jacinta an apology. She tried to hurt herself.'

'What happened?'

'You did that to her.'

'Me? How?'

'You know how.'

A dog came bounding towards us, but we didn't welcome it. A canopy of dark sky was advancing from the south. I didn't have a raincoat with me. 'Jacinta's see-sawing mental health isn't my problem,' he said.

'It is though.'

My not-even step-brother stood up. 'You of all people, Dolores.'

'I loved you, Gavin.'

'I don't have to listen to this.'

'To what?'

'To whatever balls you and Jacinta have concocted.'

'I haven't accused you of anything.'

'You've always been out to get me.'

'Have I?'

'Yeah. Both of you. And your mother. Even David.'

'That isn't true.'

'Have you told Faye?'

'No.'

'Are you planning to?'

'I have no plans.'

He made his hands into fists and rubbed the knuckles together. 'I was a kid, Dolores.'

'You were. And then you weren't.'

'I cared about you,' he said.

'I mean, for a long time I thought that's what it was.' A jogger on the path behind us ran by, her dog tied to her waist with a long lead. He watched her as she disappeared over the hill. 'But it wasn't love or care or concern or admiration.'

'What was it then?'

'Do you need me to tell you what it was?'

'This is horseshit.'

'Jacinta almost died. I almost lost my sister because of what you did.'

'What about Maya and Freddie?'

I hesitated. For a second I wasn't sure who he meant. Maya and Freddie: his children. I hadn't considered them at all – not even their safety. 'I don't know what to say about that. Or about the baby you're about to have.'

He adjusted his watch, looked at the time. 'So now what?'

I shrugged. I had no idea. It seemed improbable that I would see Gavin again, that we would be able to find a way to go back to how things were, ignoring the stench of the past and pretending to be some sort of family. 'I'll have to get back to you once I've decided. It might be a while before you hear from me.' I wanted David to be there with me at that moment. Maybe he would have hit Gavin. He certainly would have deboned him in some way. I could only feel loss.

'Fine,' he said.

'Don't contact her again. Or Mum. You aren't related to them.'

'Whatever.' He stood up and looked down at me like I was disgusting to him. I'd never seen this expression before and it scared me. I had to look away, across the park to where two small girls were picking daisies.

'Whatever,' he repeated. And he was gone.

•

I took Mum to Rottingdean for a walk along the white cliffs. She was slow and kept worrying that the seagulls would shit on her fresh blow-dry. A woman sped by on an electric bike and she screamed.

We sat at an outdoor café and watched the waves pitch against the rocks. She never mentioned Jacinta or David or asked how I was. She complained that the tea was too milky.

She said, 'Can you tell that eegit next door to stop parking across my driveway?'

'We're getting you more care, Mum. Someone to be at the house overnight.'

'I don't need a babysitter.'

'I know.'

A boy on a scooter went past, tassels on his handle-bars. A young mother chased after him. She was carrying a younger child in her arms. I wanted to ask Mum what she remembered. I wanted to know if she remembered. I said, 'You never talk about Gavin. You never call him. He rarely visits you. Why is that?'

'Gavin?' She took a sip of tea. Her fingers were so thin. Her cheeks were sunken. She looked much older than a woman in her early seventies. 'Who was he then? Gavin. Did we ever find out?'

I reached across the table, took her hand. 'Don't worry about it, Mum.'

•

David came to pick up the last of his stuff. He tried to use his key then rang the bell. 'I changed the locks,' I explained.

He came inside, slipped off his trainers out of habit.

The rugs were rolled up, most of the kitchenware packed. It had the same echo we sang into when we moved in. We called it the song of potential.

'I packed up anything I thought you'd want,' I said.

'I don't want much,' he murmured.

'We'll pay a penalty on the fixed term mortgage.'

'It is what it is.' He went to the stairs and sat on the bottom step. He hung his head between his knees and began to cry. 'I didn't mean for any of this,' he said. 'I've ruined our lives.'

The wooden floors in the hallway needed hoovering. There were square stains on the walls from where our pictures had been hanging for ten years. We never bothered to get a new front door with glass in it that would let in the light though we'd been planning to for ages. I hated the colour of the carpet on the stairs – dark green which we agreed would be forgiving. Forgiving of what? All our mistakes and spills?

'I can't go backwards,' I said. 'I wanted to for a long time. I missed you. But something's changed.'

He had been lonely for so long and I watched him slipping away without a thought to stop it happening. 'I've met someone,' he said. 'She's not like you at all. And I'm glad she isn't. But I also hate her sometimes.'

It was my turn to cry, to heave in chunks of air like they were rare and difficult to retrieve. He put an arm around my shoulder, pulled me closer. I couldn't remember when we'd last willingly sat so close.

I thought, I'll tell him. And then I thought, He shouldn't carry it. He doesn't need it in his bag of stories.

He put three boxes into his boot. I stood in the doorway until his car disappeared. I wanted his new relationship to fail, for me to be the only person he could ever possibly love. I wanted to let him go. I wanted him to be happy.

Upstairs Zoey was sitting on the bed in the spare room. I'd dressed her in jeans and a jumper. 'Hey, Zoey, are you ready?'

•

My belongings were going into storage until I'd completed on the new house. The last box was long and narrow, undeniably shaped like a coffin. 'Please be careful with this,' I said. The movers picked her up gently and carried her out to the lorry.

I called Jacinta from departures. My flight was delayed and I would miss the car transfer we were meant to be taking together from Wade International Airport to our beachfront hotel. She told me not to worry, that she'd have a drink ready for me when I arrived. She asked if I had a lot of luggage. 'Carry on,' I told her.

I paid for the priority lounge and watched other travellers checking and rechecking their gate numbers and flight times on the screen, everyone going somewhere.

I didn't know exactly what I was doing.

I ordered a glass of wine. The nicest they had. A small glass. I planned on having a couple of drinks on the flight too. Watch a film. Eat from the little plastic containers. 'Anything else I can help you with?' the waitress wanted to know. I was about to ask her for the weather forecast in Bermuda but checked myself. I'd have to remember this about real people: that they rarely have all the answers.

'Madame?' She was busy. And I was dithering.

'No, I don't think so. I think that's it,' I said.

Acknowledgements

TK

A Note on the Type

The text of this book is set in Bembo, which was first used in 1495 by the Venetian printer Aldus Manutius for Cardinal Bembo's *De Aetna*. The original types were cut for Manutius by Francesco Griffo. Bembo was one of the types used by Claude Garamond (1480–1561) as a model for his Romain de l'Université, and so it was a forerunner of what became the standard European type for the following two centuries. Its modern form follows the original types and was designed for Monotype in 1929.